"This was Adam Clinton, in a photograph taken six months before he murdered his wife and stepdaughter," the TV show's host said. *"He was twenty-nine. Thanks to advanced computer technology, we can get some idea of what he might look like today, fifteen years later."*

As she stared at the television, Livvie could hear the clunk of the quartz clock over the stove. She felt the cool flow of air from underneath the back door, and smelled the bits of tuna on her plate. It was as if all her senses were suddenly sharpened.

But her eyes were working best, as she looked at the age-enhanced photograph of Adam Clinton.

Livvie didn't know where Adam Clinton had gone in the years after the police lost his trail, but she knew where he was now.

Adam Clinton was Allen Richardson, her stepfather.

Other Point Thrillers you will enjoy:

THE STEPDAUGHTER

CAROL ELLIS

SCHOLASTIC INC.
New York Toronto London Auckland Sydney

No part of this publication may be reproduced in whole or in part, or stored in a retrieval system, or transmitted in any form or by any means, electronic, mechanical, photocopying, recording, or otherwise, without written permission of the publisher. For information regarding permission, write to Scholastic Inc., 730 Broadway, New York, NY 10003.

ISBN 0-590-46044-7

12 11 10 9 8 7 6 5 4 3 2   3 4 5 6 7 8/9

Printed in the U.S.A.   01

First Scholastic printing, April 1993

Chapter 1

Alone in her room, Livvie Palmer lifted her head from the pillow and listened.

Footsteps, coming up the stairs.

Quickly, she swung her legs over the side of the bed and sat up. It was six o'clock in the evening. She'd meant to lie down for just a few minutes, but she'd drifted into a sort of half sleep. It was so easy to do, so easy to let the time slip by that way.

The footsteps passed the spare room, hesitating at the master bedroom.

Livvie had thought she was alone in the house. But someone else was there. Someone was coming down the hall, not bothering to be quiet.

Walking like he belonged there.

The footsteps got louder, echoing off the polished wood floor. Livvie stood up. Her knees wobbled and she almost sank down again. But the footsteps were even louder. He was almost at her bedroom. In the few seconds before he reached her door, she moved swiftly and silently across the soft carpeting to the other side of the room.

He stopped just outside her door.

Livvie could picture him putting his head against it, listening. She held her breath. She heard her heart drumming loudly in her ears. Could he hear it, too?

There was a sharp rap on the door.

Livvie jumped and heard herself make a sound. Sort of a high-pitched gasp. He had to have heard it. She swept the room with her eyes, but it was too late to hide anywhere now.

The door opened and Livvie saw him. He wasn't a prowler. He wasn't a burglar or a fiend. He was just a middle-aged man with sandy, thinning hair and a pair of perpetually raised eyebrows that gave him a questioning look.

He was Livvie's stepfather, Allen Richardson.

Richardson took a step into the room, but kept his hand on the doorknob. The back of his hand had a birthmark; it looked like a tiny map of Africa. "It was so quiet in here, I thought you might be asleep," he said. "Sorry if I scared you."

Livvie shook her head. He must have heard her gasp, but she wasn't going to admit to being scared.

"Got a test?" Richardson asked, his mild brown eyes looking at the Spanish book on the desk behind her.

"Maybe." Livvie picked up the book. "I'll know tomorrow."

"Oh, your teacher threatened you with a pop quiz, huh?" Richardson chuckled. "I hated those things."

Livvie decided no response was required. She went on looking at him, her expression neutral. Her "beige" look, she called it. It went with anything. People could read whatever they wanted into it. Usually they decided you felt the same way they did.

Richardson cocked his head to one side, a habit he had. "Your mother and I are going to the Santa Fe restaurant for dinner. Well, she told you that already, I guess. Said you'd decided not to come, but I thought I'd see if you'd changed your mind."

Thoughtful. As in, "He's such a thoughtful man, Livvie, I think you'll really like him." That was one of the things Livvie's mother had said about Allen Richardson when she'd decided to remarry. To Livvie, he always seemed strangely *too* thoughtful. As if it wasn't genuine, but just an act he put on.

"They have a special on enchiladas tonight," Richardson went on. "That's your favorite, isn't it?"

"I really have to study, Allen," Livvie said, tapping the book. "I'll make myself something in a little while. Thanks, anyway."

"Allen?" Patricia Richardson's voice called up the stairs. "My stomach's growling, let's go. Livvie? Are you coming?" Livvie's mother sounded hopeful. Livvie didn't like disappointing her, but she'd gone for pizza with them four days ago, and she ate dinner with them almost every night. Her mother really couldn't complain.

"She's hitting the books," Richardson called down. He turned back to Livvie. "We'll get you some enchiladas anyway. You can have them tomorrow, if you've already eaten by the time we get back." With a broad smile he stepped out, pulling the door shut behind him.

Why was he always trying so hard? Livvie wondered. She waited until the house was quiet again. Then she sat down in the desk chair, elbows on her Spanish book, chin in her hands, eyes closed.

"Promise you'll give him a chance," her mother had said.

"Nobody's asking you to love him," her therapist had said.

"I don't expect to replace your father," Richardson had said.

Livvie opened her eyes and looked at the snapshot on the bulletin board above her desk. It was of William Palmer, her father, taken shortly before he died of a sudden, unexpected heart attack two years before. He was tall and a little overweight, with thick hair and gray eyes that Livvie had inherited. She'd loved him very much, and when he died, she'd felt lost. That was normal, everyone had said. It takes time, they'd said, there's no limit on how long you should grieve, and no rules about how. They'd said that after Livvie had stopped eating and sleeping, after she'd wound up in a hospital. Then came months of therapy with Dr. Carter; Livvie still saw her once in a while.

Livvie knew she wasn't "over" her father's death. You didn't get over something like that, you just learned to live with it.

What she couldn't live with (or, hadn't tried hard enough to live with, according to some), was Allen Richardson.

When her mother had started dating him, Livvie knew she was worried. Worried that Livvie would break down again. Talk about walking on eggshells! But Livvie had no intention of falling apart. She expected her mother to date, maybe even marry again, and she didn't see it as any kind of betrayal of her father's memory, either. She was strong again, she just wasn't strong enough to stomach the man her mother had married.

Enough. Livvie snapped off her desk lamp and stood up. How much time did she have? An hour, an hour and a half? Plenty of time to eat, watch a little television, and be back upstairs studying when her mother and stepfather came home. If she was lucky, she wouldn't have to see him again until tomorrow.

The phone rang as Livvie finished putting lettuce on her tuna sandwich. She slapped on the top piece of bread and picked up the phone. It was her friend, Marta Ryland, asking about some history notes.

"I must have fallen asleep in class," Marta said. "With my eyes open — it's a trick I've perfected. Anyway, there's this big blank space in my notebook. Did you manage to stay awake long enough to write everything down?"

Livvie smiled to herself. Marta might have missed some notes, but that wasn't her main reason for calling. Her main reason was to keep in touch, to make sure Livvie was okay. Even though they saw each other in school, Marta always called. She'd stuck by Livvie through her father's death, the breakdown, the remarriage. Through thin and thinner, as Livvie liked to call it. She was a good friend.

Livvie ran upstairs and got her history notes, then brought them back down to the kitchen and started eating her sandwich while she read them over the phone.

"Okay, got it, thanks," Marta said. "If Mr. Zimmer calls on me, I'll be ready. I hear you chewing," she added. "Are you guys in the middle of dinner?"

"Just me," Livvie said. "Mom and Richardson went out."

"Are you still calling him that?" Marta asked. " 'Richardson'?"

"Only when I'm being polite," Livvie said. She laughed; but Marta didn't. "It was a joke, Marta. Anyway, you know how I feel about him."

"How long have they been married now, a couple of months?" Marta asked.

"Two and a half."

"Right. And nothing's changed?"

"Well, Mom's happy again," Livvie said. "Look, I can't help it. I know everybody thinks he's the greatest guy to ever walk the earth — "

"Nobody said that," Marta interrupted. "It's

just that he's really nice. He has a sense of humor, he treats kids like people instead of aliens, he's . . . I don't know . . . an okay guy. Really okay."

"Yep," Livvie said.

"So why don't you like him?" Marta asked, not for the first time. "What makes you think he's the stepfather from hell?"

Livvie sighed. She really didn't want to talk about this. Besides, she couldn't put her finger on why she didn't like Allen Richardson. It was an instinctive thing, she guessed. Maybe it didn't make sense, but there it was.

"Look," Marta went on, "I'm sorry. You don't have to like him. Forget I said anything."

"It's okay," Livvie said. "I know everybody thinks I'm crazy for not liking him."

"Nobody thinks you're crazy," Marta said sharply. Then she added jokingly, "A little weird, maybe."

"That's me, all right." Livvie laughed. "Weird Olivia Palmer."

After Livvie hung up the phone, she turned on the television that sat at the end of one of the counters. Her mother said she'd always wanted to watch the morning shows while she made coffee and packed her lunch. The television was one of Richardson's first purchases after he'd moved in with them. Not a bad idea, Livvie hated to admit.

Picking up her sandwich again, Livvie settled back with the remote control and started zapping from station to station, going from game shows to talking heads and stopping briefly at a movie. A man and woman, obviously having trouble with their romance. The woman was talking about leaving him. Couples breaking up always made her think of Rob Silver. Their romance hadn't survived Livvie's problems. She'd finally decided it was just as well, but she couldn't help missing him sometimes. She changed the station.

Fugitives from Justice was just coming on. Livvie had seen it a few times. Each week, the show told about a certain criminal who hadn't been caught yet. It recreated the crimes, interviewed police, showed pictures, and ended by asking anyone who'd seen the person or had any information to call a special number. Livvie knew it was all true, but she could never quite believe it. She always felt like she was watching a made-for-TV mystery.

Tonight's crime involved a double murder. *"Murder in the Midwest,"* the host intoned. *"Fifteen years ago, the bodies of Sharon Clinton and her eight-year-old daughter Cynthia were found dead of smoke inhalation in the bedrooms of their modest house on Crabapple Lane."*

There was a photograph of a small ranch house, its white shingles charred and darkened by fire and water. The screen switched to a grainy video shot of the same house, this time with two men wheeling a gurney out of the front door. On the gurney was a small shape, completely covered in what looked like a tarp.

Livvie got up and went to the refrigerator for some milk. She didn't really want to see the bodies, covered or not. She listened while she poured milk into a glass.

"The deaths shocked and saddened neighbors and strangers alike," the host went on. *"They dreaded telling Adam Clinton, husband and stepfather."*

Livvie leaned against the counter and drank, listening but not watching. She didn't want to see people grieving outside a burned-up house, either.

"But the shock and sadness, natural when two people, one of them a child, die unexpectedly, soon gave way to puzzlement, to suspicion, and finally, to outrage," the host said. *"Just two days after his wife and stepdaughter died, police named Adam Clinton as the man who set the fire that killed Sharon and Cynthia.*

He never came back on that ill-fated night. To-day, fifteen years later, Adam Clinton is still a fugitive from justice."

The show's theme music swelled, and then a commercial came on. Livvie went to the table and looked through her history notes. When *Fugitives from Justice* came back on, she kept reading, listening to the show with one ear. Not the best way to study, but she knew most of it anyway.

"We may never know for certain, but we think he did it for the life insurance," a man's voice was saying. *"When Sharon married him, she listed him as the second beneficiary. Cynthia was the first."*

"But Cynthia was only eight," the interviewer said. *"Wouldn't Clinton have been in charge of the money?"*

"No, a lawyer would have been in charge until Cynthia turned twenty-one," the man said. *"Now, Sharon Clinton wasn't a rich woman, far from it. This was all she really had to leave her daughter, and she wanted to make sure her daughter got it."*

"Are you suggesting she didn't trust Adam Clinton?" the interviewer asked. *"And by the way, what about Cynthia's biological father?"*

Still hungry, Livvie got up and rummaged in the cabinet. While she wrestled open a package of chocolate cookies, she heard that Cynthia Clinton's biological father had died in a car accident, and that no, the police didn't think Sharon distrusted Adam. She just wanted to make sure no one misused the money she'd left to her daughter.

"*How much would Adam Clinton have gotten?*" the interviewer asked.

"*One hundred thousand dollars.*"

"*When we come back,*" the announcer said, "*we'll see what went wrong with Adam Clinton's plan, and take a closer look at the man who, for one hundred thousand dollars, murdered his wife and stepdaughter.*"

Talk about a stepfather from hell, Livvie thought, sitting down at the table again. She read some more notes during the commercials, and then shut the notebook when the show came back on. She was curious now.

Evidently, the police and fire investigators had gotten curious, too, especially when they found traces of lighter fluid on the rug in the master bedroom. Later, autopsies revealed that both Sharon and Cynthia had been drugged.

And of course, there was the especially curious fact that Adam Clinton didn't come home. He worked as a buyer for a chain of hardware stores, and he was supposedly away on a buying trip. Actually, he *was* on the trip, he'd just left a little late, after starting the fire. His plan was to get the horrified call from his boss, or hear about it on television and come racing back. But he was supposed to come racing back to a gutted house and bodies that could only be identified through dental records. He hadn't counted on the fire being spotted by a neighbor with insomnia. Once he realized there was enough evidence left to make the police extremely suspicious, he just never came back at all.

"Four days after the fire, Adam Clinton's car was found in the long-term parking lot of the nearest major airport," the host said. *"Airline personnel were able to identify a photograph of him, and a record of flights revealed that he flew to Chicago.*

"There, his trail stopped cold."

An overhead shot of O'Hare Airport faded and another picture came on the screen — a photograph of a man in his twenties, smiling at the camera. Adam Clinton. He was leaning against a tree trunk, his fingers stuck partway into the pockets of his jeans. It was a slightly blurry picture, and Livvie squinted, trying to get it into better focus. His hair was light brown and straight and it looked very fine. He had a moustache, a little darker than the hair on his head. His right hand had something on it, like a speck of dirt. As the screen changed to a close-up of his face in the same photograph, Livvie reached for her milk, not looking at what she was doing. Her hand hit the glass, knocking it over and sending a stream of milk flowing across the table. Livvie heard it splash onto the floor, but she didn't move.

She didn't take her eyes away from the television.

Adam Clinton's eyebrows were darker than his hair and they were raised. This wrinkled his forehead and made his expression puzzled, questioning, in spite of the smile. His head was tilted slightly to the right.

"This was Adam Clinton, in a photograph taken six months before he murdered his wife and stepdaughter," the show's host said. *"He was twenty-nine. Thanks to advanced computer technology, we can get some idea of what he might look like today, fifteen years later, at the age of forty-four."*

The flow of milk had slowed to an intermittent drip. Livvie could hear it. She could hear the clunk of the quartz clock over the stove and the whir of the refrigerator motor. She felt a cool flow of air from underneath the back door, smelled the bits of tuna on her plate and felt the grit of cookie crumbs on her fingers. It was as if all her senses were suddenly sharpened.

But her eyes were working best, as she looked at the age-enhanced photograph of Adam Clinton.

They'd taken away the moustache, but they still got it wrong, she thought. He was losing his hair, but not the way they'd done it. It wasn't receding from the forehead and the temples, it was just getting thinner all over, so you could see shiny patches of scalp here and there.

They'd forgotten to raise the eyebrows. Of course, they didn't know about them the way Livvie did. They didn't know his eyebrows were almost always raised, as if invisible strings were pulling them up. They didn't know that tilting his head was an unconscious habit.

Livvie didn't know where Adam Clinton had gone in the years after the police lost his trail in Chicago, but she knew where he was now. She knew what he looked like, too — a man of average height and weight. A man of average looks, with nothing distinctive about them except his eyebrows and the tilt of his head and the tiny birthmark on the back of his right hand. He sold houses for a living. He was well-liked by almost everyone who met him. Everyone except Livvie.

Adam Clinton was Allen Richardson, her stepfather.

Chapter 2

The show cut to a commercial, a loud, raucous ad for cars. Livvie stared blindly at the television for a moment as a showroom salesman frantically shouted the praises of the latest models. Then she gave herself a shake.

It was impossible.

Wherever Adam Clinton was, he wasn't living here with Livvie and her mother. He couldn't be. Livvie didn't like Richardson, but that didn't make him a killer. Maybe it was *because* she didn't like him that she was so ready to see a resemblance between him and Adam Clinton. So what if the resemblance was strong? Everybody was supposed to have a twin somewhere in the world.

The television pictures of Adam Clinton flashed into her mind again, but Livvie forced them away. Then she took a handful of napkins and started to sop up the spilled milk, keeping her ear cocked for the return of *Fugitives from Justice*. But before it came back on, she heard a jolting thud and then the rumble of the garage door as it climbed slowly up its tracks. At the same time, a car crunched over the gravel driveway, and Livvie saw the sweep of headlights across the kitchen windows. Her mother and stepfather were home.

Quickly, Livvie put away the cookies and set her plate and glass in the dishwasher, slamming the door so hard it bounced back open. She made herself shut it carefully. Then, as she heard the garage door start to close, she remembered the television.

Fugitives from Justice was back. At the bottom of the screen was the special telephone number for people to call if they had information about Adam Clinton. Above it were two pictures of him, the photograph when he was twenty-nine, and the age-enhanced close-up. Livvie froze for a second, staring at the screen.

She couldn't believe how much the pictures looked like Richardson.

Livvie shut the television off, just as the kitchen door opened, and Richardson and her mother came in.

"Hi, honey," Patricia said. "We brought you some enchiladas."

"Cheese and chicken." Allen Richardson held up a paper sack.

"Oh, well, thanks," Livvie said, distracted. She was looking at Richardson's hand, the one with the birthmark on it. Then her eyes slid up to his face.

Suddenly she saw Adam Clinton's face, as if it were superimposed on her stepfather's.

"What's the problem, Livvie?" Richardson asked.

Livvie realized she'd been staring. But they looked so much alike.

She blinked fast, forcing the image away, and said the first thing that came to her mind. "Salsa. For a second, I thought you had a piece of tomato stuck in the corner of your mouth. But it was just a shadow."

Richardson brought his hand to his mouth, and Livvie noticed the birthmark again. From where she was standing, it didn't look like a map of Africa. It looked like a speck of dried mud.

Like the one in the photograph of Adam Clinton.

Livvie told herself to stop it. They couldn't be the same man. Lots of people had moles or freckles or birthmarks on their hands. It was just another coincidence.

"Livvie, what's the matter with you?" Her

mother sounded annoyed. "I've asked you twice if you want to have some coffee with us."

"Oh. Sorry." Livvie shook her head, harder than she had to. She was trying to shake away all thoughts of Adam Clinton. "Uh, no, no coffee, Mom. I better keep studying." She waved the history notes at them, and then left the kitchen.

Upstairs in her room, Livvie tossed her notes on the bed and flopped on her stomach beside them. She knew most of the stuff already, but she'd study anyway. It couldn't hurt. And it would keep her from thinking stupid thoughts, like maybe her stepfather wasn't who he said he was.

Of course he wasn't Adam Clinton. Adam Clinton was probably in New York or Los Angeles. Someplace big, where he could be anonymous. He wouldn't be stupid enough to settle in a small town and actually get married again.

As Livvie opened her notebook, she suddenly heard the muted sound of the television downstairs in the kitchen. She sat up so quickly she could feel the blood drain from her face. She hadn't changed the station! *Fugitives from Justice* was still on, and she hadn't changed the station. Did they do a wrap-up at the end? Would Allen Richardson, sitting there drinking coffee, see his own face on the screen? Would he know that Livvie had been watching it earlier and wonder if she'd recognized him?

This was ridiculous! They weren't the same man! She was just suffering from an overactive imagination, that was all. Still, she couldn't keep herself from going to the bedroom door and easing it open.

She could hear the television more clearly now. Two men arguing, cutting each other off, their voices rising. Livvie caught the words "Democratic majority" and "Congressional ineptitude." It was a political talk show, one of her stepfather's favorites, she remembered now.

Relieved, Livvie closed her door and leaned against it. Then she made herself go back to the bed and pick up her history notes. After history, she'd study Spanish. There really was a possibility of a quiz tomorrow and it was her worst subject. And maybe if she concentrated on Spanish, she'd forget about what she'd seen on television.

She was wrong about Richardson, she had to be.

Because if she was right, then she and her mother were living with a murderer.

Chapter 3

Livvie tried to forget it. Over the next couple of days, she did everything she could to push the thoughts out of her head. But they kept pushing their way back in. She'd be sitting in class or getting herself a snack, and the picture of Adam Clinton would suddenly flash into her mind. She'd push it out. But it always came back. When it did, she'd feel exactly the way she'd felt when she first saw it. Her heart would start thudding and her hands would get clammy.

"Adam Clinton is still a fugitive from justice," she could hear the TV host say.

Could she be right? Could her stepfather be a *murderer*? If he was, did he still think about it? How did he feel when someone stared at him, or made an innocent remark, or used the expression "getting away with murder"? Did his heart start to pound and his hands get sweaty, the way Livvie's did every time she thought of it?

This is crazy, Livvie thought. She kept telling herself she was wrong. She had to be.

Livvie knew she should talk to someone. Probably saying it out loud would make the whole thing disappear.

Finally, on Saturday morning, Livvie called Marta.

"Are you crazy? Are you absolutely out of your mind?!"

Livvie flinched as she heard Marta's voice over the phone, shrill with disbelief.

"Look, I'm sorry," Marta went on in a more normal tone. "I didn't mean that like it sounded, but, my God, Livvie!"

"I know it sounds crazy," Livvie said. "But I can't help it, Marta. I swear, Richardson looks exactly like that man."

Livvie was alone in the house. Richardson was showing houses, and her mother was getting her hair cut and then shopping for shoes. According to the note from her mother on the refrigerator, neither one of them would be home until some time after lunch. She'd stared at the phone for about fifteen minutes before calling Marta, but finally she'd done it. She had to confide in someone, and her mother was out of the question.

"Listen, Livvie. I know you don't like the guy. I don't understand why, but never mind that for now." Marta spoke calmly and quietly now, like a person trying to reason with someone who was about to jump off a bridge. "But you can't accuse somebody of murder just because he happens to look a little bit like the real murderer. I mean, your stepfather's very ordinary. He doesn't exactly stand out in a crowd."

"I'm not accusing him," Livvie said. "But he looks more than 'a little bit' like Clinton."

"Which means he looks like a million other guys," Marta said. "And a million other guys look like him."

"You're saying it's just a coincidence."

"Right. Plus, even though you don't like him, he's never done or said anything to make you think he's some kind of wacko killer, has he?"

"You mean like poisoning the neighbor's dog?" Livvie asked in exasperation. "Marta, I didn't say he's this psycho serial killer who keeps on doing in mothers and stepdaughters. Maybe he just wants a regular life now. Except he wants it with *us*!"

"I thought you said you weren't accusing him," Marta reminded her.

"I'm not! I just . . . I don't know," Livvie said. "I don't know what to think."

"Livvie, come on. He's a nice man. Everybody likes him," Marta said. "Don't you think somebody like that would have a dark side or something?"

"Beige," Livvie said.

"Huh?"

"Never mind." Livvie realized that if Richardson was Clinton, then he must have used the beige look, too. Nice and ordinary, so he wouldn't draw attention to himself.

"Well, anyway, don't get mad, but I think you're totally wrong," Marta said. "Everybody who knows him thinks he's great. Your mother married him, remember? You think she's some kind of idiot? If you'd let yourself get to know him, you'd think he was great, too."

Marta paused and cleared her throat. Livvie could almost see her twirling a finger through her frizzy brown hair. Marta was working up to something. She cleared her throat again. "Are you going to talk about this with Dr. Carter?" she asked.

"Oh, Marta!" Livvie said. "You think I should see my shrink? You think I'm losing it again?"

"I didn't say that!" Marta protested. "Don't put words in my mouth. But maybe she could talk you into trying to get to know him better and giving him a chance."

"Dr. Carter doesn't talk me into doing anything," Livvie said. "She helps me talk myself into doing things."

"Well, whatever. Are you going to see her?"

"She's out of town. But maybe you're right," Livvie said thoughtfully. "Maybe I should get to know Allen better."

"Hey, you used his first name," Marta laughed. "That's a start."

After they said good-bye, Livvie took the cordless phone back into her mother's and Richardson's bedroom. Marta was right. She didn't know Richardson very well.

So why not start now? If she did get to know him — and maybe even like him — she would realize how ridiculous it was to think he was a murderer. She could forget about the whole thing.

The clock on the bedside table said ten to eleven. Livvie had an hour, probably more, before anyone came home. She glanced around the room. It was the same as when her father had been alive, except that now Allen Richardson's clothes filled the drawers and one of the closets. Livvie walked over to the chest of drawers and fingered the brass handles of the top drawer.

She knew she shouldn't be poking through his things, but she had to find out. She had to know whether she was crazy to think her step-father was hiding a secret. A horrible secret.

Livvie pulled open the drawer.

Eleven-thirty. Livvie was downstairs now, in a small room at the back of the house. It used to be for storage, but when Richardson moved in, he'd cleaned it out and put in a desk, a file cabinet and shelves, and a computer terminal from the real estate office.

Livvie had found nothing in the bedroom. She had even searched the back of the closet, hoping to find a shoebox of letters or a boot stuffed with newspaper clippings. But his past wasn't upstairs. Maybe it was here. She probably should have started here first, because he was the only one who used the room.

Starting with the desk, Livvie began to search, not sure what she was searching for anymore. She couldn't really expect to find a piece of paper that would identify him as Adam Clinton. He wouldn't be stupid enough to keep something like that all these years. He wouldn't keep news stories about the murder or his old driver's license or any kind of ID card.

Besides, she didn't *want* to find anything like

that. She wanted to find something proving he *wasn't* Adam Clinton.

As the minutes passed, and she moved from the desk to the filing cabinet and finally to the shelves, Livvie suddenly realized that she *had* found something. It wasn't proof that Richardson was Richardson. It wasn't proof that he was Adam Clinton, either. But it was something: Allen Richardson didn't have a past. Upstairs or down, she hadn't found a single scrapbook, yearbook, old bank statement, photograph, letter. *Nothing.* All Allen Richardson had brought to this house were his clothes, some tools, and a few boxes of paperback books.

Livvie was sixteen, and already she had a past — grade school pictures, a couple of ribbons from swimming, high school yearbooks, birthday and Christmas cards and valentines she'd saved.

Not everyone was a pack rat, but everyone saved something, didn't they? So why hadn't Richardson?

Was it because he'd had to erase his past?

Because if it caught up with him, it could kill him?

It was a feeling more than anything, a change in the empty atmosphere of the room, but Livvie suddenly realized she wasn't alone any longer. She jerked her head toward the door and felt the blood rush to her face.

Her stepfather was standing in the doorway.

"Hello, Livvie," Allen Richardson said. "What are you looking for?"

Chapter 4

"Allen." Livvie slowly got to her feet. "You scared me."

"I called out when I came in the house but I guess you didn't hear me."

"I guess not. I . . ." Livvie looked down at the shelf she'd been searching, trying to come up with a reason for being in the room.

"Yes?" Richardson asked, looking at her closely. "What were you looking for?"

Bending down, Livvie took a yellow notepad from a stack on the bottom shelf. "I have to go to the library and look up some stuff for a history paper," she said, holding the pad out. "I forgot to bring home my notebook, and I thought you might have something in here. Okay?"

"Sure." Richardson frowned a little, as if he didn't believe her. "Whatever you need."

"Okay." Livvie walked around the desk toward the door. "Thanks."

In the doorway, Livvie could feel his eyes watching her, knew he was wondering what her real reason was for being in his little office. But when she turned back to see, Richardson was looking at some papers on his desk, not at her. She clutched the yellow notepad and hurried down the hall.

He hadn't been watching her at all, she told herself. It was just her imagination. Or was it?

Livvie had been lying to Richardson about having to do research, but the lie gave her an idea. After she left him, she got her jacket and caught a bus downtown. If she could find a book on unsolved murders, and Adam Clinton was in one of them, she might be able to learn something that would help her. She didn't believe he could have completely changed everything about himself. There would have to be something left over from his past, a habit or hobby that he'd kept. Something *Fugitives from Justice* hadn't mentioned, but maybe a book would. Books got into lots of details like that.

At the library, she asked for the true crime section and spent half an hour looking through all the books, but finding nothing. Then she checked the card catalog in hopes that a book mentioning the Clinton murders might have been checked out. Nothing there, either.

Frowning, Livvie leaned back against the catalog and looked around. The library had once been a private house. They'd added onto it, but they'd kept the big bay windows in the main room and turned them into reading areas, with couches and chairs and low tables. A few people were in them now, most of them looking at newspapers.

Newspapers.

Of course, Livvie thought. There must have been a zillion stories about the Clinton murders at the time. If she could get copies of them, they might tell her something.

Half an hour later, Livvie left the library with the address of *The Morrisville Sun*, the newspaper from Adam Clinton's town, written on the yellow notepad she'd taken from Richardson's office.

Back on the bus, Livvie's mind was racing. She'd call the newspaper as soon as she got home. No, wait, she couldn't make a call like that unless she was alone. She didn't want to be overheard. Anyway, wouldn't the call show up on the telephone bill? Yes. Okay, she'd have to write and ask for copies of the articles. But what if Richardson got home early and picked up the mail, like he sometimes did?

The bus lurched to a stop, jolting Livvie in her seat. The jolt brought her back to reality. What did she think she was doing? Why was she planning to get information about Adam Clinton? He and Richardson couldn't be the same man. She should be trying to learn more about her stepfather, to find out something — anything — that would prove he wasn't Clinton. She probably still wouldn't like him, but at least she'd be able to stop thinking about that stupid television show.

As the bus pulled away from the curb, Livvie unzipped her bookbag and took out a small spiral notebook. What did she know about Richardson, except that he didn't keep stuff from his past? He'd moved here from California four years ago, he'd said. He'd never married; a big romance with a high school sweetheart had fizzled. He was a good handyman. He sometimes wore glasses.

Livvie looked at what she'd jotted down. Then she drew a line down the middle of the page. In the second column, she listed what she remembered from the television show about Adam Clinton. Then she compared the two.

They were hardly a match. The two men looked alike, to Livvie, anyway. That seemed to be all. She stuffed the notebook back in her bag and closed her eyes. When the images of Adam Clinton appeared, she snapped her eyes open and stared out the window.

"You're being awfully quiet, Livvie," Patricia Richardson said on Monday night. "Are you feeling all right?"

Livvie glanced up from her dinner of chicken and vegetables. "I'm okay," she said. "Just kind of tired. We're doing this national physical fitness stuff in PE and Ms. Fremont just about ran us into the ground." She wasn't really tired, but it was a good excuse for being quiet.

"I know that feeling," Richardson said. "I remember working out for football until I thought I'd drop."

Something about what Richardson was saying struck her as strange, although she wasn't quite sure why. For one thing, he didn't seem big enough to have played football. But there was something else . . .

Then she remembered.

It was the first time her stepfather had taken Livvie and her mother out for dinner, and somehow the subject of sports had come up. Livvie's mother had asked if he'd played any when he was younger.

"Sure did," he'd said. *"Led my team to the state championships."*

"In what sport?" Livvie had asked.

"I was on the soccer team."

Livvie could remember it so clearly, because she played soccer, too, and her mother had suggested that maybe she and Richardson could work on her shooting and passing sometime.

She was sure he'd said *soccer* that day. And how could he be on the soccer team *and* the football team, which both competed in the fall?

"Weren't you on the soccer team?" Livvie asked. "You took Mom and me to dinner once, before you got married, and you said you'd played soccer."

"No — I think I said I wished I had," Richardson said. "But no, it was football. Of course, I only made the second string."

"Oh." Livvie wasn't sure she believed him. "What position did you play?" she asked.

"Bench warmer." Richardson laughed and reached for the platter of chicken.

A non-answer, Livvie thought. "This was in high school, right?"

He nodded.

"In California?"

Richardson took a bite of chicken and nodded again.

"Is that where you were born?" Livvie asked.

He put his fork down slowly and looked at

her. "What is this, Livvie? An interrogation?"

His lips were smiling, but he wasn't amused. Even through his glasses, Livvie could see that his eyes were serious. Serious and cool.

"Yes, Livvie," her mother said, breaking into the silence. "Stop asking so many questions and give the man a chance to eat."

"It's all right." Richardson was still looking at Livvie. "I just can't help wondering why you're suddenly so interested in my life story." His stiff smile widened. "You never were before."

Livvie managed a slight smile in return. "I was just curious, that's all," she said.

"Nosy is more like it," her mother said. "Now, come on, let's finish dinner."

Richardson gazed at Livvie for another beat. Then he picked up his fork and started eating again. Soon, he and Livvie's mother were talking about something else.

Livvie pushed the food around on her plate and glanced at her stepfather. He hadn't answered Livvie's question about where he was born. Had he forgotten she'd asked?

Or did he just not want to answer?

As Livvie looked at him, Richardson took off his glasses and rubbed his eyes.

"Headache?" Livvie's mother asked.

"Mmm," Richardson said. "I think it's time to have the prescription changed."

Livvie wanted to ask him why he had them on at all. He said they were reading glasses. Why was he wearing them to eat?

She didn't ask. She'd already asked too many questions. And her stepfather's reaction had been odd.

That's what made her finally decide: she'd write the newspaper. She couldn't stop thinking about it, no matter how hard she tried.

Livvie mailed the letter on Tuesday. She put Marta's address on the return envelope. Once she'd done it, she felt silly.

It just wasn't possible that the man her mother married had killed two people, one of them his own stepdaughter.

That stepdaughter's name was Cynthia. Livvie remembered the picture she'd seen of her on television. If Cynthia had lived, she would have been older than Livvie was now.

Somehow Livvie felt connected to her. Had Cynthia had the same feelings about Adam Clinton that Livvie had about Allen Richardson? Had she instinctively disliked him? Had everyone wondered what her problem was, the way they wondered about Livvie? Had she gone to bed at night wishing her mother had never brought this man into their lives?

Chapter 5

Livvie kept watching Richardson. She couldn't help it. He didn't say anything, but she knew he noticed.

Her mother noticed, too. Livvie knew her mother was unhappy that she hadn't welcomed Richardson into their home with open arms, knew she was waiting and hoping for the day Livvie would realize what a wonderful man he was. Up to now, Livvie had been careful not to complain, not to be rude, not to say anything that would start an argument. Only Marta knew how she really felt about her stepfather. But now, being distant but polite was getting harder and harder. She thought she was keeping up a pretty good act, though, until a couple of days after she'd written to the newspaper, when her mother knocked on her bedroom door, wanting to talk.

"About what?" Livvie asked, suddenly

afraid her mother wanted to have a heart-to-heart about Richardson.

Patricia Richardson sat on the bed where Livvie was lying, her Spanish book propped against her knees. "About spring vacation," she said. "It starts next week."

"I know and I can't wait," Livvie said.

Her mother looked down and started smoothing the bedspread. "Livvie, I can't help noticing how edgy you've been for the past week."

"Well." Livvie shifted around on the bed, trying to think of what to say. "Well, we're having all these tests right before vacation, you know. Everybody gets kind of antsy."

"Oh, I understand," her mother said. "But you've been more than antsy, Livvie. You — now please don't get defensive — but you've gotten so tense and quiet. Allen's noticed, too. And I can't help worrying about you."

"Yeah, well. Don't, okay?" Livvie should have known her mother would think she was heading for another breakdown. And if her mother knew the real reason Livvie was so tense, she'd really think Livvie was out of her mind. "I'm fine, really, Mom. Just tired of school. Ready for a break."

Her mother didn't look completely convinced, but she obviously decided not to push it. With a smile, she said, "Well, that's great, because a break is exactly what you're going to get. We all are." Her blue eyes sparkled with excitement. "Do you remember Joanne Ward?"

"Umm . . ."

"No, of course you don't," Patricia laughed, "you were only a baby when you met her. She and I were best friends in high school and we've always kept in touch. Anyway, she got divorced about a year ago. She and her three kids live in this run-down old house in Cliffside, right near a lake. Joanne wrote me that the house needs a lot of repairs, and contractors cost a fortune."

Livvie hadn't figured out where this was going, so she just smiled and tried to look interested.

"Anyway," her mother went on, "that's what we're doing for spring vacation."

Livvie stared at her. "Fixing their house?"

"No, we're going to visit them!" her mother said. "Allen's going to do some repairs for her, but basically we're going to lounge around and go boating for two whole weeks! Doesn't that sound great?"

"Sure, but — "

"I know, I know, you're worried about the kids," her mother said. "Don't. Two boys and a girl, nineteen, seventeen, and fifteen. You'll fit right in. And the house is a huge old monstrosity, with enough bedrooms for an army. There'll be plenty of privacy. Oh, Livvie, it'll be good for you. For all of us," she added quickly. "We could all use a vacation."

Livvie got it now. Besides wanting to see her old friend, her mother wanted to make sure Livvie didn't fall apart again. So she'd arranged a nice, restful, lakeside vacation. It might have been fun, Livvie thought, except for Allen Richardson. But maybe in another place, with a bunch of other people, it wouldn't be so bad. He'd be doing repairs and she could spend her time at the lake.

Now Livvie had to tell Marta what she'd done. She'd been putting it off, but since they were going away, she had to tell her to expect something from *The Morrisville Sun*. Marta came over two days before school let out for the break, and after they'd studied history for a while, Livvie decided she couldn't put it off any longer.

"I'm thirsty," she said, scooting off the bed. "Do you want a Coke?"

"I just finished one." Marta was lying on the rug, notebooks spread out around her. "So did you, you know. You'll turn into the stuff if you keep drinking it."

"Okay, I'm hungry."

"What you are is sick of history." Chin in her hands, Marta grinned. "So am I. I'll take whatever you can find."

"Be right back." Livvie left the bedroom and hurried down the hall, checking into both of the other rooms before going downstairs. She wasn't hungry or thirsty. She just wanted to make sure the house was still empty.

Downstairs, she looked into Richardson's office, then hurried back to the kitchen. She made sure the door was locked, so she'd hear him if he came in. Then she went back upstairs.

Marta glanced up when she came in. "Where's the food?"

"Oh." Livvie glanced at her empty hands. "I forgot."

Marta's blue eyes were skeptical. "What did you go down there for, anyway? I heard you moving around like some kind of prowler."

"I need to tell you something," Livvie said. Leaving the door open, she crossed to the bed and sat down. "It's about Richardson."

"Oh." Marta sat up, cross-legged, and immediately started twisting her hair around a finger. "Listen, I guess you wonder why I haven't talked about what you told me," she said. She glanced at the open door and lowered her voice. "About . . . you know."

"Yes, I know," Livvie said. "Don't worry. He's not here. He's at work."

"Livvie, you're not still seriously thinking about that show?" Marta asked.

"Yes, I am," Livvie said. "That's why I wanted to talk to you. I need a favor." She was quiet for a moment, listening for sounds from downstairs. When she didn't hear any, she explained about the letter she'd written to *The Morrisville Sun*. "So if anything comes while we're away, could you send it to me? Only put it in another envelope, so he won't see the real return address."

Marta was staring at her openmouthed.

"Don't look at me like that," Livvie said. "I told you I was serious."

Marta closed her mouth and stared at the rug. After a minute, she said, "I know you did. I guess the reason I haven't said anything about all this is because I was hoping you weren't." She looked up, her hair all tangled, her eyes pleading. "Livvie, I'm sorry. I just can't believe what you said about him."

"I'm not sure I do either," Livvie said.

"Then why'd you write the newspaper?"

"To find out for sure. Because I can't stop thinking about it," Livvie said. "The two guys look alike, I told you. And I went through his stuff . . ."

"You *what*?"

Marta was looking at her like she was crazy, but Livvie kept on talking. "I looked through some of his things. Marta, he hasn't kept a single thing from his past. No pictures, no letters, nothing. I'm not kidding. That's just not normal."

Marta still looked skeptical. "So why don't you just go ahead and call the police?"

"Because I'd have to be sure!" Livvie cried. "You know what would happen if I called them. The whole thing would be out in the open. There'd be questions and investigations. It's like it would come alive and I couldn't stop it, even if I was wrong. So I have to be sure."

"But you're not sure," Marta said. "You said you're not sure."

"One minute I am and the next I'm not," Livvie said. "Can't you understand?"

Marta shook her head.

"Okay, you don't have to believe me," Livvie said angrily. "I guess I can't expect you to. But please, don't worry about my mind. It's perfectly clear, okay?"

Marta nodded.

Livvie took a breath. "Sorry. I didn't mean to get mad. It's just . . . if I can't talk to you about it, then I don't have anybody to talk to."

"Okay."

"So will you do it?" Livvie asked. "Send me the stuff about Adam Clinton if it comes while I'm gone? I'll give you the address in Cliffside."

"Sure." Avoiding Livvie's eyes, Marta started gathering up her notebooks and papers. "Listen, I think I'd better get going. It's getting late and it's my turn to fix dinner tonight."

Usually, Marta would have invited Livvie to come and help and stay to eat, but she didn't this time. Livvie knew why. Marta was uncomfortable. She might be Livvie's best friend, but she didn't want to hear any more wild talk about Allen Richardson.

It made Livvie sad, knowing Marta didn't believe her, possibly thought she was losing it for good this time. But as she wrote down the Cliffside address, she shook the sadness off. At least Marta had agreed to send the information, if it ever came. Maybe that was all she could expect for now.

"Here," she said, handing Marta the piece of paper she'd torn from her notebook.

Marta took it and stuffed it in her jeans' pocket. She still didn't meet Livvie's eyes. "See you tomorrow."

"Right. Thanks, Marta." Livvie sighed as she watched Marta leave the room, then she sat on the bed again, staring at her notes. She heard Marta trot down the stairs, then she heard her say, "Oh, hi, Mr. Richardson."

Livvie froze for a second. Richardson must have just come in. She must not have heard him because she and Marta were talking. But she would have heard him if he'd come up the stairs, wouldn't she? He couldn't have come up and listened and then gone back down — or could he?

Marta and Richardson were talking. Livvie heard Marta laugh, then stop and say something in a lower voice. Richardson seemed to ask a question. And Livvie suddenly felt icy cold and panicky. Was it possible that Marta was telling him everything?

Livvie knew she should go down and break up the conversation, but she couldn't move. She sat there, still and frightened, wondering if her best friend was betraying her.

Chapter 6

The town of Cliffside, where the Wards lived, was about a two-hour drive away. They left early on Saturday morning, taking two cars, because Richardson had said he might have to make a trip or two back home to show houses. Livvie's mother and Richardson took his car, and Livvie followed in her mother's. Livvie hadn't been driving very long, and she'd never driven far from her own familiar streets, so she kept a close watch on the car in front.

On Thursday, after her first few moments of panic, Livvie had finally gone downstairs and walked in on the conversation between Marta and Richardson. They were talking about school and tests, not about Livvie's suspicions. Then again, they might have changed the subject when they heard her on the stairs. But Livvie made herself believe they hadn't. Wondering about her stepfather was bad enough.

She couldn't let herself get paranoid about her best friend, too.

About a half hour or so outside of town, the scenery changed. Suburban housing developments, all neat and rectangular, gave way to rolling hills thick with trees just beginning to turn green. The highway climbed so gradually that Livvie didn't realize they were actually in the hills until they came into the town of Cliffside. The small downtown, with several stores and a few old houses converted into offices, was on a flat stretch of road. But the homes where most people lived were stacked up on the hills, circling three sides of the town and overlooking a silvery lake ringed with trees. It was a beautiful place, and for a few moments, Livvie let herself pretend they were a happy family, going on vacation.

The Ward house was on a narrow, winding street. Pulling into the drive behind Richardson's car, Livvie saw two people, a tall teenaged boy and a middle-aged woman, standing next to a motorbike, one on either side of it. They were obviously arguing. Their hands slashed through the air, and even with her window closed Livvie could hear the shouting. At the approach of the two cars, they both turned their heads, and Livvie saw that the boy's face was red with anger. He said something to the woman and then hopped on the motorcycle, gunned the engine, and tore down the drive, spewing up gravel and almost sidewiping Livvie's front fender.

"I'm so embarrassed!" the woman was saying as Livvie got out of the car and joined her mother and stepfather. She recognized the woman as Joanne Ward from pictures her mother had shown her. "What a horrible welcome! Kyle's gone now, so why don't you turn around and drive back in and I'll come running out with a smile on my face, like I'd planned?"

She laughed and hugged Livvie's mother, and the two of them shrieked about each other's hair and how good they both looked. Livvie remembered that Kyle was nineteen, the oldest of the three kids. The others were Joel and Dana, seventeen and fifteen, her mother had said. She didn't see them anywhere. She hoped they were in better moods than Kyle.

"So you're Allen!" Joanne said, giving him a hug, too. "I'm thrilled to meet you." She stepped back and smiled at him. "You're just like Patricia described you, and I can tell by the way she looks that you've been wonderful for her."

"It's mutual, Joanne," Allen Richardson said a bit too smoothly, Livvie thought. He reached for Patricia's hand and squeezed it.

Livvie gritted her teeth and felt her pretense fade away. Even if he wasn't Adam Clinton, they weren't a happy family, not while Richardson was part of it.

Joanne Ward turned to Livvie then, and more shrieks followed as she said how much she'd grown, how pretty she was, what lovely gray eyes she had. "Well," she said, when she'd finished complimenting Livvie, "let's go in. Now don't expect luxury," she warned with a laugh. "We've got space, but that's about it."

Looking at the house, Livvie saw what she meant. It was big, all right, three stories high with a wraparound porch and a turret on one corner. The house had once been yellow, but most of the shingles were faded and cracked, and there were rust stains where water leaked from broken gutters. The porch boards and railing were peeling white paint, and one of the steps was broken completely. Only the front door looked good, freshly painted in shiny red.

"I know you won't believe it after his performance a few minutes ago," Joanne said, opening the door, "but Kyle actually volunteered to paint the door for me." She sighed and shook her head. "That was before he decided to be as belligerent as possible. I don't know what's the matter with him. Lately we argue all the time. Oh, well, don't let me get started on that!"

The front door opened into a small, dark entryway with hooks for coats and narrow benches for sitting down to take off your boots. Two glass-paned doors opened up into the house itself. They went into a wide hall with a stairway off to one side. A boy with brown hair and sunglasses was coming down, his hands stuffed in the pockets of his jeans.

"Joel, they're here," Joanne said. "Come say hello."

Joel Ward stopped and shook hands as his mother made the introductions. Instead of taking the sunglasses off, he slipped them down to the tip of his nose and peered over them. His eyes were almost the same shade as his hair, Livvie noticed, a kind of chestnut brown.

"Olivia," he said, when his mother introduced them. He said her name slowly, in a deep, full voice, like a Shakespearean actor.

"Don't get carried away." His mother tapped him on the arm. "She likes to be called Livvie. At least," she said, turning to Livvie, "I think that's what you like."

"It doesn't matter," Livvie said, smiling at Joel. He was cute, she decided. She liked the way he'd said her name.

Joel smiled back and turned to his mother.

"Is it safe to venture outside now? I heard the monster roaring."

"Oh, that motorcycle," Joanne said, rolling her eyes. "I swear I'm going to take a sledgehammer to it someday."

"I meant Kyle," Joel said.

Livvie laughed.

"Your brother's gone, if that's what you mean," Joanne said to Joel. "And where's Dana, by the way?"

"The princess didn't confide in me," he said. "But if I had to guess, I'd say the lake."

Joanne clucked her tongue. "All right, then you're elected to help get their bags inside while I'm showing them their rooms."

"That's what I'm here for," Joel said. He shoved his sunglasses up and went outside.

"He's a sweetheart," Livvie's mother said as they filed up the staircase.

"Compared to Kyle, he's a saint," Joanne said. "What an awful thing to say! Anyway, Joel's been a bit touchy since his father left, so don't be surprised if he's moody once in a while."

Listening, Livvie felt even more drawn to Joel. They'd both lost their fathers, in different ways. She could understand why he might be moody.

"That's understandable," Richardson said, echoing Livvie's thoughts. "He must feel two ways about the divorce — knowing it's probably for the better, but wishing it never had to happen. And I'm sure he can't help missing your husband."

"Oh, yes, that's exactly it," Joanne agreed. She poked Patricia in the back. "Talk about sweethearts," she whispered.

Richardson was doing it again, Livvie thought. Being Mr. Nice Guy, saying all the right things. He'd only been here fifteen minutes and he already had Joanne Ward singing his praises. Was it just an act? Or was that really who he was? Maybe *she* was the one playing a role — the bitter stepdaughter.

Dana Ward showed up while Livvie was checking out her room on the third floor near the back staircase. It had faded wallpaper, a low ceiling, and windows that overlooked a cement patio surrounded by a low brick wall. Livvie was kneeling at one of the windows, watching a gray cat slink along the top of the wall, when she heard someone say, "Hi."

Turning, Livvie saw a pretty barefoot girl with long blonde hair and a turned-up nose. She was wearing a sweatshirt and cut-offs and two earrings in each ear. "I'm Dana," she said, leaning against the doorframe. "Mom said to come introduce myself."

"Hi. I'm Livvie." Livvie hoped introducing herself wasn't a chore for Dana. She'd never really thought about how the Ward kids might feel, having three people suddenly descend on their house. "Come on in. Have you been to the lake?"

"Yes, and it's freezing!" Dana said, plopping onto the bed. "Too cold to swim, but we took a boat out." She held up a bare foot. "I lost a shoe. They were expensive — Mom's going to kill me." Without waiting for Livvie's response, she said, "You're sixteen, aren't you?"

Livvie nodded.

"You can drive, right? I can't wait till I can. My boyfriend Kevin has been teaching me." She leaned back on her elbows. "Of course, I don't know *what* I'll drive. We only have one car and Mom uses it most of the time."

"How about Kyle's motorcycle?" Livvie suggested jokingly.

"Are you kidding? He'd kill me if I touched it. He's such a creep." Dana shook her head and sighed. "It's too bad Mom and Dad split up. We have zero money."

Livvie tried to look sympathetic.

"Maybe Mom'll get married again, like yours," Dana said. "I met your stepfather. He said I could borrow his car while he's here, but then Mom told him I'm not sixteen yet." She fiddled with one of her long feathery earrings. "He's going to fix our roof, did you know that? For nothing!"

"It leaks?"

"Buckets," Dana said. "You're lucky. I mean, forget about the money, your stepfather just seems like a really nice guy. I love my dad and all, but I don't think he'd fix somebody else's roof like that."

"Yeah, well . . ."

"Anyway, I've got to go over to my girl-friend's now, but I'll be back for dinner," Dana said, getting up. "We can make plans for to-morrow. We all hang out at the lake most of the time. I'll introduce you to everybody." Tossing her hair back, Dana left the room.

Livvie turned to the window again. The cat was still on the wall, washing its face now in the sun. Suddenly it stopped, its paw in the air, its eyes wide as it looked at the back of the house. Livvie heard voices and laughter. Her mother and Joanne. Then Richardson came into view on the patio, talking over his shoulder to the two women. The cat stood up and stared at him for a second, its back arched. Then it slipped like a shadow over the wall.

It seemed to Livvie the cat had the same instincts about Allen Richardson as she did.

Chapter 7

"It's a *terrific* house," Richardson gushed at dinner. "The basement doesn't leak as far as I can tell. Some of the wiring looks pretty ancient, but I think I can help out with that. Except for the roof, it's basically sound, so you can relax." He patted Joanne's hand.

"You've made my day, Allen," Joanne said, toasting him with her glass of wine.

Disgusted, Livvie watched Richardson playing the role of the "sweetheart," as Joanne had called him. Couldn't they see what a fake he was?

"The basement doesn't leak?" Dana asked skeptically. "How come it's so damp and smelly then? It stinks like a sewer."

Livvie silently agreed. In fact, the house gave her the creeps. Richardson had asked for a top-to-bottom tour, and Livvie had gone along. There were supposed to be a couple of secret passages, but Joanne wasn't sure where they were, and Livvie was just as glad. Small, dark places made her claustrophobic. The attic was hot and dusty, but the basement was horrible. There was only one area big enough to stand up in, and it was taken up mostly by a furnace with long vents that snaked along the ceiling like square arms. The rest of it was mostly cobwebby crawl space, and Dana was right, it smelled like a sewer.

"It's because of the dirt floor," Richardson was saying. "And not enough ventilation. Cement and another window or two would help, but they're not necessary."

Livvie tuned him out and snuck a glance at Joel. He was sitting across the table from her in the dining room. He was twirling spaghetti on his fork, his eyes on Richardson, but Livvie got the feeling he wasn't really listening either. As if he could feel her watching him, he shifted his gaze to her and gave her a mysterious little smile.

Livvie grinned and drank some lemonade. Maybe he'd be an ally here. Dana was friendly, but she talked mostly about herself, and when she didn't, she talked about her big crowd of friends. Livvie thought there must be about a hundred of them, and she'd never been much of a crowd person.

As for Kyle, Livvie decided she'd try to avoid him as much as possible. He was good-looking, if you liked the brooding type, but he had a definite attitude problem. She'd heard Joanne telling her mother that he went to the community college, but spent more time hanging out with a couple of drop-out friends than he did studying. Livvie hadn't seen him smile yet.

No, that wasn't true. He'd smiled twice. Once when he'd come home and Richardson asked him about the motorcycle. "Got it secondhand, but it runs great," he'd said. "Why, you want to take it for a ride?" And he'd smiled tauntingly.

"Well, I haven't been on one of these since my high school days," Richardson had said. "But sure, I'm game." And he'd hopped on the bike and peeled off down the driveway. When he came back, Kyle smiled again, this time with surprise and pleasure. "Not bad for . . ."

"An old man," Richardson finished. He laughed and handed the helmet back to Kyle. "Thanks, it brought back memories."

Now, at dinner, Kyle finally broke his silence. Turning to Richardson, he said, "You wouldn't know anything about engines, would you? My bike's had this ping in it, maybe you noticed."

Richardson started to answer, but Joanne broke in. "Now, Allen, you don't want to get started on that hunk of metal," she laughed. "You'll never get a chance to see the lake if you do."

"Right, like you don't plan to have him up on the roof the whole time he's here," Kyle said.

"Kyle, I was just joking!" Joanne looked flustered and annoyed. "Allen offered to help with the roof, as a friend. I don't plan to *make* him do anything. He can do nothing and I'd still be glad to have him here. To have them all here."

"Sure, right." Kyle angrily tore off a piece of garlic bread.

"You make it sound like I'm taking advantage," Joanne said.

"I think I can probably find time to take a look at the bike," Richardson said smoothly.

"Forget it." Kyle scraped his chair back and stood up.

"Where are you going?" his mother asked.

"Out." He tossed the uneaten bread down and left the room. A moment later, they heard the roar of the motorcycle.

"Now he'll be gone for hours," Dana said. "And he promised he'd drop me off at Sherry's house."

"Sherry lives two streets down," Joanne told her. "You can walk." She looked around the table and then clapped her hands on her head. "I guess I said the wrong thing to him, as usual. I apologize."

"Don't," Livvie's mother said. "Raising one child is hard. Raising three must be — "

"Hell," Joanne said with a laugh. "No offense, kids," she added. "Oh, well, I guess I shouldn't complain too much. I can remember a few years when I was impossible to live with."

With that, she and Livvie's mother were off, talking about being teenagers together. Dana excused herself and left for her friend's house. Everyone had finished eating, so Livvie gathered some plates and took them into the kitchen. She was putting a stack on the counter when she heard the swinging door open behind her.

Joel was there, carrying some glasses and nudging a cast-iron, turtle-shaped doorstop with his foot to keep the door from swinging shut again. "Easier this way," he explained, bringing the glasses over. "You really don't have to earn your keep," he said, setting the glasses next to the plates. "I can clear the table."

"No, that's okay," Livvie said. "That's not why I'm doing it. I just felt like it."

"Not interested in the talk about the olden days?"

Livvie smiled. "Not really."

"I guess we'll be hearing a lot of it while you're here," Joel said, putting the plates in the dishwasher. "We'll have to try to escape early and come back late. Did the princess work you into her crowded social calendar?"

"I'm going to the lake with her tomorrow," Livvie said, laughing. "Do you always call her that?"

"No, sometimes I call her monster," Joel said with a straight face. "But I call Kyle that, too, and then they both answer. It confuses them." He smiled. "I'm just teasing them. Usually. Don't you do that?"

"I don't have any brothers or sisters," Livvie explained. "I call my mother Wonderwoman sometimes, when she's trying to do fifteen things at once and won't admit she can't."

"What about your stepfather?" Joel asked. "Got any nicknames for him?"

Livvie opened her mouth and shut it. Frowning a little, she shook her head.

Joel looked at her. "Oh. Bad question, huh? Sorry."

"It's all right," Livvie said quickly. "I just . . . he's not . . ." she stopped, embarrassed.

"Forget it." Unlike Kyle, Joel said the words gently. "We'll stay off the subject. Ice cream?"

"What?"

"Do you want ice cream?" he asked, going to the refrigerator. "That's what we're having for dessert. Dessert's a safe subject, isn't it?"

Livvie laughed. "Yes, and yes I like it. Tell me where the bowls are."

When she and Joel brought the ice cream into the dining room, the two women were still reminiscing about their teenage years, and Richardson had joined in. "Her name was Mrs. Simwit," he was saying. "Naturally, we called her 'Dimwit.' She was the terror of Chesterfield high. In fact, I think she was the terror of the whole town of Chesterfield, maybe the entire state."

Joanne laughed. "She must have been awful, to terrorize all of California."

"No, this was Iowa," Richardson said. "Tiny town, just a dot on the map."

"Iowa?" Livvie put a bowl down in front of him. "You never said anything about Iowa."

Richardson looked up at her. Livvie saw his eyes change, the way they had when she'd questioned him at dinner that time. But she knew she was right, he hadn't mentioned going to high school in Iowa.

"You remember," she said. "You were talking about football. It was just a few days ago."

Richardson shook his head. "I guess my memory's getting bad," he said. "I don't remember any discussion about football."

"It wasn't exactly about football," Livvie said. "I was tired from PE and you said you used to get tired working out on the team. The high school team. You said it was in California."

Livvie looked at her mother, but Patricia was busy scooping out chocolate ice cream and talking to Joanne. They weren't paying any attention. Livvie looked back at Richardson. "You didn't mention Iowa," she said again.

"Well, I must have forgotten," he said. "You're not going to hold that against me, are you?"

"You forgot going to high school in Iowa?"

"That's not what I meant." Richardson's eyes were still flat and cool. But his voice rose a little. Joanne and Patricia stopped talking and looked at him. Livvie waited.

"I could hardly forget about Iowa, Livvie," Richardson said, bringing his voice back to normal and chuckling softly. "I moved to California in my junior year. Before that, I was in Iowa. I just forgot to mention it." He turned to the two women and changed the subject.

Livvie sat down and dished out some ice cream for herself. Twirling it around in the bowl to soften it, she looked at her stepfather. She hadn't imagined the way his eyes changed. He didn't like to talk about his past. He didn't like her asking questions about it. Why? Why would he care?

Unless he had something to hide.

While she stared at her stepfather, the face of Adam Clinton flashed into Livvie's mind. Clinton, with his head tilted and his eyebrows raised. Just like Richardson. The two faces seemed to merge, and Livvie blinked. This time, the image didn't go away.

Livvie looked down at her melting ice cream. Now someone was staring at *her*, she could feel it. She took a deep breath and looked up, sure it was Richardson.

But it was Joel. His rich brown eyes, darker than her stepfather's, were watching her intently.

Chapter 8

Livvie shivered as she walked with Dana to the lake the next day. She had her new swimsuit on under her jeans and sweatshirt, but she didn't think she'd get a chance to break it in.

"It's always cold during spring vacation," Dana said. "It'll probably warm up some, it usually does. The water's still icy, but we go in at least once. Most of the time we just hang out on the beach or take a boat out."

"Do you have a boat?" Livvie asked.

"Yeah, this old, beat-up rowboat," Dana said, wrinkling her nose. "My dad was talking about getting a canoe, but I guess it'll never happen now."

"Can you waterski on the lake?"

"No, the swimmers started complaining about the waves and the noise and pollution and everything, and the town decided to ban powerboats." Dana looked cross. "Kevin bought a jet ski just before it happened and now he can't use it. It was really great. Joel says they're ugly and noisy, but he's never tried one. All he does is row out to the middle and sit there by himself." She shrugged. "Joel's weird."

"Is he? He's kind of cute, though," Livvie said.

"Yeah, I guess." Dana looked at Livvie. "He used to be a lot of fun. But now he's always wandering around, thinking. By himself," she added, as if being alone qualified somebody for weirdness. "Sometimes he's funny and joking and then suddenly he'll get all quiet and wander off. Mom says it's because of Dad, but Dad moved out three months ago. And he calls and we'll be seeing him over the summer. It's not like he died or anything. Oops, sorry," she said. "I forgot about your father. Your real one, I mean."

"It's okay," Livvie said. "I guess Joel just misses your dad."

"Yeah, well, that's okay," Dana said. "But you can miss somebody without becoming a totally different person and acting weird about it." She shook her hair back and changed the subject. "Do you have a boyfriend?"

"Uh, no, not now."

"Well, you'll meet lots of guys at the lake,"

Dana told her. "Kevin has a couple of friends who aren't going with anybody right now. I bet one of them will like you."

Livvie kept quiet. The question was, would *she* like one of them?

They crossed the main street of Cliffside, and Livvie followed Dana along a narrow path between two buildings and down a steep cement stairway onto the rocky beach. There weren't many trees along that part of the lake, and a few picnic tables had been set up. Two wooden piers jutted out into the water, tied-up rowboats and canoes bumping gently against them. Thick rope ringed off a shallow swimming area, and way beyond that was a square aluminum platform with a ladder climbing up the side.

"The lake gets really deep out in the middle," Dana explained. "You can dive from the platform."

A crowd of kids was on the platform, their rowboats tied to the rungs of the ladder. Dana waved and shouted and one of the guys stood and waved back, rocking the platform and causing everyone to shout at him. "That's Kevin," Dana said, her expression proud and possessive.

The kids scrambled from the platform into the boats, and after a few minutes of rowing, they pulled up at one of the piers, where they piled out and raced along the beach to Livvie and Dana. With Kevin's arm around her shoulders, Dana introduced Livvie to her friends. "And this," she said, wrapping her arm around Kevin's waist, "is my boyfriend, in case you hadn't figured that out. Kevin Russo."

"Hey, Livvie." Kevin was blond-haired and square-faced, not very tall but with a thick chest and muscular legs in tight jeans. His blue eyes traveled quickly up and down Livvie's body and he smiled as if the two of them shared some kind of secret.

Livvie said hi and looked away fast. Dana might think he was hers, but Livvie had the feeling that Kevin didn't tie himself to any girl for long.

"We brought some stuff," Dana said, holding up the duffel bag she was carrying. "Soda and pretzels and stuff. But let's go out in the boats first, okay, Livvie?"

"Sure." Livvie walked along with the group back to the docks, and soon found herself in a rowboat with Kevin's two friends, the ones who were unattached at the moment. David and Lloyd. Lloyd rowed and David joked about how slow he was. Dana's friend Sherry was with them, a small girl with long dark hair and eyes for David. They all seemed nice enough, but

Livvie couldn't help feeling like the stranger she was. She trailed her hand in the cold dark water and looked toward the shore, wondering if Joel would come to the lake today.

She wondered, too, about Richardson's story last night about Chesterfield, Iowa. He'd been lying, she was sure of it. Maybe there was such a place, but she didn't believe he'd ever set foot in it. He'd probably just read about it and worked it into his background, forgetting that he'd told Livvie and her mother he'd gone to high school in California. That's if he was Adam Clinton, of course. But if he wasn't, then why would he lie?

Richardson had never mentioned the name of the California school, but Livvie suddenly realized she could check on Chesterfield. It was a tiny town, he'd said. It probably only had one high school. If she could get in touch with them, she bet she could prove his lie.

Was she getting carried away? Livvie wondered. Well, she'd already written the Morrisville newspaper, so what difference would a little more investigating make? No one needed to know.

Unless. Unless she turned out to be right about Allen Richardson.

Later, after they'd eaten and drunk everything in sight, the group started to look for something else to do. Some wanted to go to the movies, others had to get home. Kevin and Dana, along with Lloyd, David, and Sherry, decided to go to a mall about twenty miles away. "We can get some pizza there," Dana said to Livvie, "and just hang out until we have to go home."

Livvie looked at her watch. It was only one, and even though there wasn't much to do back at the house, she didn't really feel like hanging out at a mall for two or three hours, especially with people she didn't know very well. Especially with Kevin, who kept looking her up and down whenever Dana wasn't watching.

"Dana, I think I'll just head back to the house," Livvie said. "I've got some reading to do over vacation." It wasn't a complete lie — she *had* brought some books, even if they weren't schoolbooks.

Dana didn't seem to care one way or the other. "Okay. Well, will you tell Mom where I've gone?"

Livvie said she would, and waved as the others started walking to a small parking area down the shore. Then she turned and climbed the steep steps back up to town. Coming out onto the main street, she heard the roar of an engine and saw Kyle on his motorcycle, another guy riding behind him. He pulled into a parking space up the block, and as he got off the cycle, he caught sight of Livvie. She raised her hand, kind of tentatively, and was surprised when he waved back. She watched him and his friend go into a place called The Green, then crossed the street and kept walking back to the Wards' house.

Joanne Ward was in the kitchen making sandwiches. "Oh, Livvie, hi. How was the lake?"

"It's really nice," Livvie said. "Oh, I'm supposed to tell you, Dana went to the mall with some of the others."

"Don't tell me they didn't invite you."

"Oh, yes, they did," Livvie assured her. "I just didn't feel like going. Don't worry about it."

"Okay, I won't. Did Joel go with them?"

"No. Well, actually, I don't know for sure," Livvie said. "Maybe he met up with them someplace, but he wasn't at the lake."

Joanne sighed. "I haven't seen that boy all day. Or Kyle either, for that matter."

"I saw Kyle," Livvie said. "Just a few minutes ago, in town. He was going into a store. The Green."

Joanne laughed, but not as if she was amused. "Well, at least I know where he is. Your mother's out on the patio, by the way.

We've been sitting out there catching up. I'm taking these sandwiches up to Allen. He's been working for hours in the attic without a break." She picked up a thermos and the plate of sandwiches and bumped open the door with her hip. "Your stepfather is just a dream," she said as the door swung shut behind her.

Just a dream. Livvie wished that were true.

The smell of ham and mustard lingered in the kitchen, and Livvie realized she was hungry. She found the bread and ham and made herself a sandwich and sat at the round table, eating and thinking. If she managed to get in touch with somebody at Chesterfield high school, what would she say? Hi, my stepfather said he went to your school, and I think he might be a murderer so could you tell me if he's lying?

She'd have to come up with a good reason for calling. If old records even existed, looking them up was going to be a pain in the neck. They might not want to do it at all.

And where would she call *from*? Livvie looked around. There was a phone in here, but she couldn't call from it, there was too much chance of being walked in on. A cordless phone would be perfect; she could take it to her room. Maybe they had one.

Livvie finished her sandwich and rinsed the

plate, then left the kitchen and went in search of another phone. And a phone book.

She found both in the living room, but as she was pulling the phone book out from its shelf in an end table, she found something else: Richardson's glasses. They were on top of the end table, lying on a couple of sheets of paper from his real estate office. Livvie figured he must have called to check on a sale or something, and left his glasses here when he went to the attic.

Looking quickly around, Livvie picked up the glasses and held them to her eyes. They were smudged, so she wiped them on her sweatshirt, then looked through them again.

Livvie didn't wear glasses, but she'd looked through other people's and every time she had, things looked blurry.

But not with these. With Richardson's glasses, the view through the front window was crystal clear. She moved them away from her eyes, then back again.

"Spying on someone?" a voice behind her asked.

Chapter 9

Livvie whirled around to face Joel, who was standing in the archway of the living room. His sunglasses were in place again, but he slid them down and frowned mockingly at her over the top. "I'm surprised, Olivia. Don't you know you can get a much more exciting view through their window at night, when the lights are on?"

Livvie laughed, more from relief than anything. Thank God it hadn't been Richardson. "I was just curious," she said, putting the glasses back where she'd found them. "You know, you see somebody's glasses lying around and you pick them up and look through them."

"Umm." Joel walked over to her and peered out the window. "See anything interesting?"

"Not really."

"Yeah, you can't see into the Mackeys' window very well from here," he said. "The view from my room's much better." He turned and smiled at her. "Just kidding. How'd you like the lake?"

"I loved it," Livvie said. "It's great being able to just walk down to it, isn't it?"

Joel nodded. "I just came from there. I thought I'd see you and Dana's crowd, but everyone's gone."

"Dana and some others went to the mall," Livvie said. "I didn't feel like it."

"Well, if you're down there tomorrow, maybe I'll see you."

Livvie wanted to suggest that she and Joel go together, but she remembered what Dana had said about how he liked to be by himself a lot. She decided to let things stay the way they were. "That'd be nice," she said. "Listen, do you have a phone?"

Joel looked pointedly at the one on the end table.

"I mean a cordless one," Livvie said with a laugh. "I want to make a call, but it's kind of private." Great, now he probably thought she wanted to call her boyfriend. "Marta," she said, wanting to set things straight. "That's my girlfriend at home. She's checking the mail for me and I'm expecting something. I want to find out if it came."

"Top secret stuff, huh?" Joel pushed his sunglasses back up. "You're in luck. Mom has a cordless phone in her room. Come on, I'll get it for you."

Livvie followed him up the stairs, across the landing, and down a hallway on the other side of the house from her room. As they walked, they passed the room with the turret. She'd dropped out of the house tour yesterday before she'd seen it. It was small, but the curved, windowed side made it special, like it was part of a castle. There was a guitar hanging on one of the walls, and Livvie stopped. "Whose room?" she asked.

"My room," Joel said shortly.

"It's great," Livvie said. "Who plays the guitar, you?"

There was no answer.

Livvie had been looking at the guitar. Now she looked at Joel. "Do you play it?" she asked, thinking he hadn't heard her.

Joel stared at her. "Does it matter?"

Even behind his sunglasses, Livvie could see that his expression had changed, hardened somehow. "No, it doesn't matter, I just . . ." she stopped. She felt guilty without knowing why. What was wrong with him? All of a sudden he looked so mean. "I just wondered, that's all," she finished.

Joel stared at her a beat longer. Then he turned away. "Nobody plays," he said as he walked on.

Geez, Livvie thought. Dana was right — he did shift moods kind of fast.

Up ahead, Joel went into a room off the hall and emerged seconds later with a white cordless phone. "You're in luck again," he said. His grim expression was gone. "It's all charged up. Sometimes Dana uses it and doesn't put it back," he explained.

"Okay, thanks." Livvie took the phone and started back down the hall. At the landing, she stopped. "I think I'm lost."

Joel came up behind her and put his hands on her shoulders. "Across the landing," he said, leaning down slightly so his head was next to hers, "then down that hall to the end and you'll meet up with the back staircase."

Livvie was very conscious of his touch and the nearness of his skin. She didn't want to move away. In fact, she realized she felt like leaning back against him. Just as she realized it, Joel lifted his hands from her shoulders. "See you later, Olivia," he said.

Livvie knew she was blushing, so she just raised her hand and walked on. "Later," she called back without turning her head.

Back in her room, Livvie crossed to the bed

and sat down, her face still warm. Maybe she'd just imagined that icy moment outside Joel's room, because there sure hadn't been any ice between them a few seconds ago. Smiling, Livvie lay back and realized she still had the phone in her hand.

She sat up and thought a moment. She wasn't ready to call Chesterfield yet. She told Joel she was going to call Marta, which was a good idea, anyway. Maybe the stuff had come from *The Morrisville Sun*. Maybe Marta would read it to her and it would blow away all her suspicions.

Livvie got up and shut the door. It must have been swollen or something, because it didn't shut tightly, but maybe that was better. She could hear Richardson thumping and hammering in the attic and would know if he quit. She didn't want him overhearing this conversation.

Back on the bed, Livvie flipped the phone's button to talk and dialed Marta's number.

Her luck was holding — Marta answered. "Hi," Livvie said. "I'm calling from beautiful Cliffside, my home away from home."

Marta laughed. "How is it?"

"Okay so far," Livvie said. "I was at the lake today and practically got hit on by a guy who happens to be the boyfriend of the girl whose house I'm staying at."

"Cute guy?" Marta asked.

"I guess. Not my type, though, especially if he likes to flirt with somebody else while his girlfriend's standing right next to him." Livvie bunched her pillow behind her and leaned back. "There's a cute guy right here in the house, though."

"Maybe I should come visit," Marta said. "Didn't you say there are two of them?"

"Yeah, but one of them has a grudge against the world," Livvie told her.

"And you've got dibs on . . . what's his name?"

"Joel. No, I don't have dibs on him," Livvie said. "He's just fun to think about, you know."

"Right."

"Well. So." Livvie cleared her throat. "Did I get any mail?"

"That's why you called, isn't it?" Marta asked. "I knew that's why you called. The answer's no."

"I guess it's too soon." Livvie knew Marta was annoyed, she could hear it in her voice, but she had to tell somebody. "I took a look through Richardson's glasses today," she said.

"I'm not sure I want to hear this."

"Please, Marta," Livvie said. "Just listen, okay?"

Marta sighed, but she said okay.

"They're just glass," Livvie said, lowering her voice. "Clear glass. Don't you see? They're a fake. Like a disguise. As if he only wears them to make him look different than he used to." She started to mention Chesterfield high, but Marta interrupted her.

"Livvie. You don't know anything about glasses." Marta sounded like she had her teeth clenched. "Maybe he doesn't wear them for regular reasons — I mean, maybe he's got a muscle problem in his eyes or something. Or just one eye. There could be a hundred reasons why they look like plain glass."

"He uses them for reading," Livvie said. "Just the other day he said he needed a new prescription."

Marta jumped on that. "Right, so maybe his eyes have gotten worse, and the glasses he has now are real weak."

Livvie had been so sure the glasses had been fake. But now she wasn't. Maybe Marta was right. "Well, anyway, will you send me the stuff when it comes?"

"I said I would and I will." Marta sighed again. "And I'll put it in another envelope, don't worry."

"Thanks, Marta."

"Yeah. Go have fun, why don't you?" Marta suggested. "Grab Joel and go wild."

Livvie laughed and said good-bye, glad that they'd ended the conversation on a happy note. She was glad she hadn't called Chesterfield, too. It was better to wait.

She started to push the button to the off position, but before she did, she thought she heard a click on the line. She held the phone up to her ear. The dial tone sounded. She pushed the button, slid off the bed and started for the door.

It didn't register until Livvie was at the door, reaching for the handle. Then it hit her like a fist in the stomach.

The house was quiet.

The hammering and banging had stopped, and the house was completely silent.

Chapter 10

It didn't have to be her stepfather.

Livvie stood with her hand on the doorknob, listening to the silence, and told herself it didn't have to be Richardson she'd heard clicking off the line. It could have been her mother, or Joanne. Or Joel.

Could it have been Joel? She'd told him she needed to make a private call. Maybe he got curious. Maybe his joke about spying on the neighbors wasn't a joke. She was attracted to him, sure, but she hardly knew him. He might be a snoop. She didn't want to believe it, but it was better than believing her stepfather had been listening in on her conversation with Marta.

The house was still quiet, though. Richardson wasn't taking a nap in the attic, so he must have come downstairs sometime while she was on the phone. There was only one way to find out where he was, so Livvie made herself pull the door open and step into the hall.

The silence continued as Livvie crossed to the narrow back stairway and started down, one hand on the shaky wooden banister. The house didn't feel deserted, though. It felt full, as if all the people in it were holding their breath, waiting.

Reaching the back landing, Livvie started down the hall toward the front of the house, past Dana's room, decorated with rock posters and stuffed animals, and the closed door of Kyle's room.

At the front, she turned and walked past Joel's room. The door was open, but he wasn't inside. She still hadn't heard any sounds except the soft plop of her own sneakered footsteps and the squeak of the floorboards.

Walking down the other hall, she went into Joanne's room, spotted the base for the phone on the bedside table, and put the phone into it. As she came back into the hallway, the house came alive.

From somewhere in the house, Livvie heard her mother and Joanne burst into laughter. Then there was the roar of a motorcycle, and a moment later, the front door slammed. Livvie heard the rumble of voices below, followed by loud laughter. "Kyle, is that you?" Joanne's voice called out.

"Yeah, I've got Ted with me," Kyle shouted. "We're hungry."

"Well, fix yourselves something," Joanne said. "And I want to talk to you later."

There was more laughter, which faded a bit as Livvie heard Kyle and his friend walk heavily toward the kitchen.

Livvie went to the front landing and started down the stairs. Allen Richardson was at the bottom, just starting up. Livvie froze. Her mind raced as she tried to remember everything she'd said on the phone to Marta. Everything her stepfather might have heard.

Richardson was climbing toward her. "Livvie. I haven't seen you since this morning," he said. "Did you have a good time at the lake?"

"Fine."

Richardson was dressed in workclothes, jeans, and an old sweatshirt with the arms cut short and unraveling. His sandy hair was covered with a thin coating of gray dust. And he had his glasses on.

"You're staring at me," he said suddenly.

Livvie jumped. "Sorry. I didn't . . ."

"I know, I look like a walking dustmop," Richardson said. "Putting an attic fan in is pretty messy work. I'm on my way to take a shower." He edged past her, going up the rest of the steps and out of sight.

Livvie stayed where she was, looking after him. The glasses had been in the living room, right near the telephone. Which meant, of course, that sometime not long ago, Richardson had been right near that telephone, too. Had he been listening in?

Hearing a sound below, Livvie turned her head and saw Joel crossing the entryway downstairs, coming from the direction of the living room. Could *he* have been the one on the phone?

She sat down on a step and propped her chin in her hands. She was starting to doubt what she'd heard. Maybe neither one of them had been listening in. It was possible that the click she'd heard was only interference on the line or something like that. Livvie knew what Marta would say: "You're being paranoid."

Well, Livvie supposed that was possible, too. But she had good reason to be feeling paranoid. Her stepfather might be a killer.

That evening after dinner, Livvie sat on her bed with the telephone book on her lap. She'd decided to call Chesterfield. Whether she was wrong or not, she had to find out, just like with the newspaper. It was too late to call now and she wouldn't have done it that night anyway, not until she was positive Richardson wasn't around. At dinner he'd said he might have to go home for half a day on business. She hoped he would; she'd call then. But for now, she could at least get the area code so she'd be ready.

She was flipping through the pages, looking for the area code section, when there was a tap on the door. Without waiting for an invitation, Dana pushed the door open and came in. "Look," she said, holding up a foot. "New sneakers. I haven't shown them to Mom yet, but I don't think she'll complain much, since they were on sale."

"Nice," Livvie said. "Did you find them at the mall?"

Dana nodded. "You should have come. Lloyd really liked you."

Livvie's mind was still on her stepfather, and for a second she didn't know who Dana was talking about. Lloyd. Oh, right, the one who was rowing.

"So did David," Dana went on, "and Sherry's not too thrilled about that. But don't worry, she's not his type, anyway."

"Wait a minute," Livvie protested. "Who says he's *my* type? Or Lloyd either?"

Dana looked surprised. "You mean you didn't like them?"

"Well, sure, I liked them," Livvie said.

"Oh, good, because they *are* pretty cool."

"Umm. It's just that we're not going to be here that long, you know." Livvie didn't want to come right out and say she wasn't interested. She didn't know *why* she didn't want to come right out and say it, except that she guessed it might be rude. "It would be awful to get really involved, you know, and then have to say good-bye."

"Yeah, I know what you mean." Dana came over and settled herself on the bed. "Kevin's on the football team and every time they have an away game, I feel like he's gone forever. I'm glad football's over." She smiled. "What'd you think of *him*?"

"Kevin? Oh, he's cute," Livvie said. She tried to think of something else. "I can tell he plays football. He's really . . ."

"Built." Dana grinned. "Tomorrow's our three-month anniversary."

"Great."

"Yeah. We're going to a movie tonight," Dana went on. "Mom asked if you were coming, but I said you didn't want to. You don't mind, do you? It's kind of a celebration. Well, for me," she added. "Kevin doesn't know I keep track of how long we've been together. He'd think it's sappy."

"I don't mind. Really," Livvie said. "I'll just hang out and read." She patted the phone book, then realized it was pretty ridiculous reading material.

But Dana didn't notice. "Great, thanks," she said, hopping off the bed and going to the door. "We're probably all going to the lake tomorrow, okay?"

"Sure. Have fun tonight," Livvie said.

"Don't worry, we will!" As Dana turned to go through the door, she almost bumped into Joel. "Geez, Joel, I didn't hear you. Why didn't you say something? You're always creeping around like some kind of zombie."

"Hey, nice to see you, too, princess. I'm here as a messenger, actually. The light of your life has arrived." Joel bowed from the waist and waved Dana out the door with a sweep of his arm. Then he turned to Livvie. "Do zombies creep?"

"I thought they kind of walked around real stiff-legged," Livvied laughed. "But maybe those're mummies."

"Well, Dana doesn't care, anyway," Joel said, lounging in the doorway. "Did she forget about herself long enough to explain why she didn't invite you to the movie?"

"You knew?"

He nodded. "I figured when she said you

didn't want to go, she hadn't bothered to ask. She doesn't like to share Kevin, not on a date, at least."

"It doesn't matter," Livvie said. "I probably wouldn't want somebody tagging along on one of my dates, either. I told her I'd hang out and read or something."

"That's what your stepfather said."

Livvie looked at him. "He said I'd read?"

"Well, no, but he said he wasn't surprised you didn't want to go to the movies," Joel explained. "He said you were kind of a loner sometimes."

"Oh."

Joel shifted his weight and leaned against the other side of the doorframe. "Could I ask you something?"

"I guess." Livvie braced herself for a question about Richardson and why she didn't seem to like him when he was such a nice, understanding guy. "Go ahead."

"Are you planning to read the telephone book?"

Livvie looked down at the phone book, laughing and trying to think of a clever answer. When she looked back up, the door was shut and Joel had vanished.

He might not be a zombie, Livvie thought, still smiling, but he sure did have a habit of appearing and disappearing without a sound. In spite of her doubts about him, about whether he'd listened in on her phone call, she still liked him. She wished he'd stayed longer.

After a moment, Livvie re-opened the phone book and found the area code section. Iowa had three of them. There was a listing of some of the cities and towns, but Chesterfield wasn't on it. But when she called information, if she got the wrong area code, they'd probably tell her the right one.

Sticking her hand under the mattress, she pulled out a pencil and her little notebook, the one she'd written in on the bus coming home from the library. She almost hadn't brought it with her. But at the last minute, she'd decided to pack it. She hadn't written in it since that time on the bus, but now she had a couple of things to add about her stepfather. If she turned out to be wrong, she'd burn the whole thing. In the meantime, she kept it hidden.

Opening it up, she made a note about Richardson's glasses, then wrote the words "Chesterfield High, Iowa." She was glad Marta couldn't see this. Marta already thought she was losing it, and this would just make her more sure.

But Marta had never seen the look in Richardson's eyes when he was asked about his past. Marta hadn't seen the face on *Fugitives from Justice.*

Marta didn't have to worry about whether she was living with a murderer.

Livvie was copying the three area codes into the notebook when she heard a muffled pounding on the back stairway. She stopped writing and listened.

Was Richardson repairing something? It was nighttime now, but Livvie wouldn't put it past him. He was so busy proving what a good guy he was, he'd probably hammer away until midnight.

But it wasn't hammering she heard. It was getting louder now. By the time Livvie realized that someone was running heavily up the stairs, the footsteps had reached her door.

There was one loud knock — a fist, Livvie was sure — and then the door was shoved open.

Kyle stood framed in the doorway.

"Do you always stick your nose into other people's business?" he asked. Livvie had never really seen him without a frown, but this was different. Kyle was furious. His hooded eyes seemed like dark lasers, boring into her.

He looked dangerous.

"Well?" he demanded.

"What are you talking about?"

"Right," he said, his voice heavy with sarcasm. "Like you don't know."

"I *don't* know!" Livvie said. "Why don't you just tell me instead of making me guess?"

"Fine. I'm talking about The Green. Remember that place? Come on," he said, advancing a few steps into the room, "it was only a few hours ago. You remembered it long enough to come running back here and snitch about it, right? Think a little, it'll come back to you."

"I saw you go in there," Livvie said. "And when I got back here, your mother was wondering where you were, so I — "

"So you opened your flapping mouth and told her," Kyle finished.

"Look," Livvie said, trying to keep her voice calm. "I didn't 'snitch,' I was just trying to . . . never mind. I still don't know what the big deal is, but if I got you in trouble or something, I'm sorry."

"Oh, 'if I got you in trouble, I'm sorry!'" Kyle mimicked in a high voice. "Nice try."

"Get out." Livvie got off the bed and faced him. "Just go, would you? I don't know what you're talking about, and I don't care. You come barging into my room — "

"*Your* room? Since when is it your room?" Kyle came a step closer. "You don't belong here. You're the one who should get out." He leaned close until his face was just a few inches from Livvie's. "You'd better watch out," he whispered, his eyes glittering. "Because trouble's what *you're* going to get."

"Just get out!" Livvie shouted.

Instead, Kyle laughed. "What's the matter, I *scare* you?"

Livvie didn't move either, and for a few seconds the two of them stared at each other. Livvie finally decided *she'd* get out.

But the minute she took a step toward the door, Kyle backed up and blocked it with his arm. "Going somewhere?"

Livvie tried to duck under his arm, but he was too quick for her, and lowered it to block her again. "Why don't you jump over it?" he suggested. He must have thought the idea was hilarious, because he started laughing again.

"What's the joke?" Allen Richardson asked, suddenly appearing in the doorway.

Kyle dropped his arm. "Private," he said. "Right, Livvie?"

Livvie didn't answer.

Allen Richardson's eyes flitted quickly over both their faces. Livvie knew he had to realize she was upset, but she wasn't about to explain. All she wanted was for them both to go.

"Well, it must have had quite a punch line,"

Richardson said after a moment. "Kyle, I thought you and I could take a look at that engine if you want to."

"Sure, that's a good idea," Kyle said.

"Okay, let's take the cycle into the garage and see what we can find." With another quick glance at Livvie, Richardson turned away and headed for the stairs, Kyle followed him.

Livvie took a deep breath and let it out. She was just about to shut the door when Kyle suddenly reappeared. He didn't say a word. He didn't have to. Cocking his thumb and forefinger like a gun, he pointed it straight at Livvie. The message was perfectly clear.

Chapter 11

"The Green? It's a bar, why?" Dana asked the next day as she and Livvie walked to the lake again.

"Well, Kyle's nineteen, right?" Livvie said. "You have to be twenty-one, don't you?"

"Yeah, but he doesn't drink in there. He plays pool." Dana rolled her eyes. "I don't know why anybody would want to go to The Green, though, it's a real sleaze joint."

"Maybe that's why your mother doesn't like him going there."

"She's not exactly thrilled with bars at all, but that's not the reason," Dana said. "See, the guy who runs it sells drugs. Everybody knows it. He's just never been caught. Anyway, Kyle did some drugs for a while, and when he stopped, Mom told him he had to stay away from that guy. She blamed Kyle for taking drugs, but she blamed the guy, too, you know? And Kyle promised he wouldn't have anything to do with him anymore."

"Oh, now I get it," Livvie said.

"Get what?"

Livvie told Dana what had happened the night before.

Dana shook her head. "No wonder Kyle was mad. Mom's probably ready to kill him."

"Actually, I think he's ready to kill me," Livvie said. "And I'm not kidding." She was a little annoyed at Dana's reaction. "Anyway, I wasn't snitching, I just mentioned the stupid place because your mother wondered where he was. How was I supposed to know it was forbidden territory?" Remembering Kyle's face, livid and furious, Livvie shuddered.

"Yeah, Kyle can get pretty out of control sometimes," Dana said.

"He practically threatened me." Livvie told her. "No, he *did* threaten me. He said I was in for trouble." Livvie took a deep breath. "I'm sorry, Dana. He's your brother — I guess I shouldn't be complaining about him to you. It's just that he scared me."

"Yeah, well." Dana paused, as if looking for the right words. "He can be creepy sometimes. If I were you, I'd keep out of his way till he cools down." Livvie couldn't help noticing an edge of tension — almost fear — in Dana's voice.

That was exactly what Livvie planned to do, anyway. Kyle hadn't been around at breakfast, and Livvie hadn't mentioned his blowup to anyone else. Richardson knew something was up, of course. But he didn't know what, and she certainly wasn't going to confide in him. When she and Dana had left the house, he and Kyle were in the garage, working on the motorcycle. The two of them made a perfect combination, Livvie thought. Or a lethal one.

"It's warmer today," Dana said, breaking into Livvie's thoughts. "Did you wear a swimsuit?"

"Yes." Livvie followed Dana down the steep steps to the beach. "But I'm not sure I want to get it wet. The lake felt pretty icy yesterday."

"I know, but it's fun, especially if you have a guy help you warm up afterward." Dana giggled and hopped over the final two steps, then ran toward the group of kids who'd already gathered near the lake's edge.

The kids were stripping off their jeans and tops, Livvie noticed, as she followed more slowly. All of them. Deciding she didn't want to be the only chicken in the bunch, Livvie shrugged and pulled her sweatshirt over her head.

The lake was no warmer than it was yesterday. As the water hit Livvie's thighs, she gasped and felt herself breaking out in goose bumps. Everyone else was gasping, too, and shrieking as they waded farther out into the lake. Livvie finally decided wading was torture. Taking a deep breath, she dove forward and started swimming for the float, which was everyone's goal. Swim out, swim back, and do it fast or you'd turn blue. Or catch pneumonia.

Livvie was a strong swimmer, and she covered the distance quickly. As she bobbed up next to the float, she tossed her hair out of her eyes and saw Kevin Russo reaching his hand down to give her a lift. Teeth chattering, Livvie grabbed onto his hand and hauled herself up, out of the freezing water and onto the slippery float.

"Thanks," she said, sluicing water out of her hair.

"Any time." Kevin grinned at her. "Pretty nice."

"Thanks." Livvie wrapped her arms around herself. "I used to be on the swim team."

Kevin chuckled. "Well, you're a pretty good swimmer, but that's not what I was talking about."

Livvie had been watching the others, some of them swimming toward the float, a couple still wading. Now she looked back at Kevin and saw that he was looking at her new swimsuit. No, not her swimsuit, her body. His eyes traveled up to her face, and he grinned again.

Great, Livvie thought. Dana's about three feet away and he doesn't even care. She wasn't looking forward to going into the water again, but it was the only way back to shore. And it was better than standing around with this guy. For a second, she felt a little sorry for Dana. With Kyle for a brother and Kevin for a boyfriend, the girl was hemmed in by jerks.

Kevin started to say something — not about the weather, Livvie was sure — but she didn't give him a chance to get the words out of his mouth. She took a couple of steps to the edge of the platform, raised her arms, and dived into the water. It was a sloppy dive, and she hoped she'd drenched him.

Back on the shore, Livvie raced toward the duffel bags she and Dana had brought, took a big beach towel from one and wrapped herself in it, head included. She hopped up and down, shivering and cold, but by the time the others had come back, she was starting to warm up. It was a clear day, and the sun actually felt hot after a while.

As she saw Kevin and Dana walking toward her, Livvie thought about going back to the house to escape him. But Kevin must have gotten her message, because he didn't even look her way. Instead, he pulled Dana into the circle of his arm and said something that made her giggle. After getting their towels, they wandered off toward the parking area. That was fine with Livvie. She turned to Sherry, who'd walked up next to her.

"What did Kevin say to you?" Sherry asked, rubbing her long hair with a towel. "He came on to you out there on the platform, didn't he?"

"Um . . ."

"Don't worry, Dana didn't see it," Sherry assured her. "She was swimming."

Livvie put her sweatshirt on. "Was it that obvious?"

"Yeah, but I could have guessed, anyway," Sherry said. "Kevin does that all the time. He thinks he's irresistible."

"Doesn't Dana notice?"

Sherry shrugged. "I guess not. She'll notice when he drops her. He does *that* all the time, too." She tossed the towel down and pulled a sweatshirt over her head. "I want to warn her, but it'd be a waste of time. She's crazy about him."

"But if he's dropped girls before, then she must know he's not exactly the loyal type," Livvie said.

"I know, but she thinks she's the one he'll stick with. You know what it's like when you're in love."

Livvie didn't know, exactly. She thought she'd loved Rob, but that hadn't lasted. Love was supposed to last, wasn't it?

"Well, anyway," Sherry went on, "like I said, I won't tell Dana about Kevin coming on to you. And don't you tell her, either. She wouldn't believe you. She'd just think you were the one who came on to him, and she'd be furious."

"That would make it two out of three," Livvie said.

"Huh?"

Livvie shook her head. "Nothing, I was just thinking. Anyway, I'm not going to tell Dana about him." If Sherry was right, she thought, Dana would find out what Kevin was like soon enough. Besides, Dana had been nice to her, in her own way, and Livvie didn't want to be the one to make her unhappy.

* * *

Kevin and Dana rejoined the group about thirty minutes later. Livvie thought they'd gone for a make-out session in his car, and maybe they had. But they'd also gone to the store and brought back sandwiches and six-packs of soda. After devouring a sandwich, Livvie decided to go back to the house. Kevin seemed to be on his best behavior, but she was getting cold and wanted to take off her swimsuit, which had never completely dried.

Up on the main street, she glanced quickly in the direction of The Green. Kyle's motorcycle wasn't there. Well, he'd be pretty stupid to go back the day after his mother chewed him out, Livvie thought. She just hoped he wasn't at the house. She wanted to avoid Kyle Ward as much as possible.

Kyle and her stepfather must have finished working on the cycle, because the garage was empty. Two of the cars were gone, Livvie noticed, her mother's and the Wards'. Richardson's car was still there, but the house was quiet when she stepped inside. Maybe he'd gone with her mother. If she could be sure he wasn't here, she might make the call to Chesterfield.

"Hello?" she called out from the entrance hall. "Anybody here?" She cocked her head and listened. No one answered. She walked into the kitchen, which was empty, then to the back of the house and looked out at the patio.

Kyle was just emerging from a little storage shed out back, carrying a hammer, a saw, and a bunch of other tools. He was heading for the back door. Livvie hurried down the hall and into the dining room, where she stayed until she heard Kyle pounding up the stairs.

He must be helping Richardson up in the attic, she thought. Paying him back for helping with the motorcycle, or just trying to get on his mother's good side. Whatever the reason, Livvie knew Richardson was here, and even if he was far above her, sweating away in the attic, she wasn't taking any more chances. She'd call Chesterfield when she was positive he was gone.

Livvie could hear some hammering now, and she figured Kyle wouldn't be back down right away. She trotted upstairs to her room, grabbed her bathrobe and shampoo, and went down to the second floor to take a shower.

After a hot shower, Livvie wrapped herself in her white bathrobe and stepped out into the hall. The bathroom was close to Joel's room, and through his open door, she could see the guitar hanging on the wall.

Without giving it any thought, Livvie went into his room and took the guitar down. She played a little, not well, but she could pick out a few chords if she tried hard enough. And it was kind of a shame to see it up there on the wall with nobody in the house able to play it.

Sitting on the bed, Livvie bit her lip in concentration and tried a chord. Disaster. She tossed her wet hair back and tried again. Better. Now for another one. Not too good, but not a disaster, either. Give her about five years and she might be able to play a tune.

Livvie was trying to remember the fingering for another chord and getting nowhere when she realized someone was standing in the doorway. She looked up, expecting Kyle. She'd forgotten about him in her feeble attempt to make music.

But it wasn't Kyle. It was Joel.

Livvie smiled, embarrassed. "Pretty awful huh?" she said. "If you had a dog, it would probably be howling right now."

Joel didn't laugh or smile back. It took a second for Livvie to realize that he was angry. Not angry like Kyle, red-faced and sneering, but a still, cold anger that was just as frightening.

"You didn't have any way of knowing about

Kyle and The Green. So that wasn't your fault," Joel said quietly. He pointed at the guitar. "But you *did* know about that."

Livvie rested the guitar on her lap. "What do you mean? All you said was nobody played it."

"I didn't mean no one was *capable*," Joel said. "I meant no one had permission. I would have told you if you'd asked. But you didn't."

While he spoke, Livvie was remembering the way he'd said "nobody plays," and how his mood had switched so quickly from light to dark, as if a cloud had blotted out the sun for a moment. She should have known enough to stay away, she thought, but it was too late.

Livvie laid the guitar aside and slowly stood up. "I'm sorry," she said. "I wasn't thinking."

"No. You weren't." Joel was staring at the air above her head. He wasn't wearing his sunglasses, and his eyes were as cold as his voice.

Livvie wished he'd look at her. There was something between them, some kind of warmth, wasn't there? She knew she hadn't imagined it. If he'd just look at her, maybe she could say something that would make him remember.

But Joel didn't take his eyes off the space above her head. Livvie knew he was waiting for her to leave. She felt like some kind of criminal, and she wasn't sure why, but now wasn't the time to ask for an explanation. She started toward the door, and he moved aside stiffly to let her pass.

Kyle and Joel, she thought as she left the room.

Now it was two out of three.

Later that afternoon, dressed in a blue cotton sweater and cut-offs, Livvie went out to the patio to let her hair dry in the sun. She sat on the low brick wall, a can of iced tea beside her, feeling a little angry. What was the deep, dark secret that was bothering Joel? She probably shouldn't have touched his stupid guitar without permission, but that was no reason for him to treat her like he had. She wished she hadn't apologized to him.

A car door slammed, and then another, and Livvie heard the voices of her mother, Richardson, and Joanne Ward. Her mother and Joanne had been shopping, she heard, and Richardson had been back home, trying to close a deal on a house. She thought he'd been upstairs the whole time, with Kyle. Now she'd wasted a chance to call Chesterfield *and* messed up her relationship with Joel.

The gray cat she'd seen the day before leaped silently onto the wall beside her. "Hi, kitty," she said. The cat ignored her and sniffed the iced tea can, then sat down to wash its face. Livvie was reaching out a hand to pet it when Dana burst out the back door. The cat gave them both a dirty look and left. Maybe it didn't like anyone, Livvie thought, not just Richardson.

"Hi," Dana said, joining Livvie on the wall. Her blonde hair was still wet.

"Don't tell me you guys went swimming again," Livvie said.

"Yeah, it was crazy," Dana said. "Everybody's lips turned blue. Listen, we're going to have a cookout tonight on the beach, okay?"

Livvie wasn't in the mood. Still, it would be better than hanging around at the house with two guys who were mad at her. She tried to smile.

"What's the matter?" Dana asked. "It'll be fun. A fire, hotdogs, marshmallows, music. Boys."

Livvie sighed. "Sorry, Dana, I know it'll be fun. I'm just in a lousy mood. I keep doing the wrong thing and now Joel's mad at me."

"Well, I warned you. Joel's weird." Dana fingered her damp hair. "He blows hot and cold. One minute he's nice and the next he makes you feel like he'd like to kill you. And he doesn't bother to tell you why." She shook her head again. "Personally, I think he's really losing it."

Livvie was quiet. She wondered if Dana was exaggerating Joel's mental state.

"I have the feeling that you kind of like him," Dana said. "Am I right?"

Livvie nodded. "I told you I think he's cute. I think he's pretty funny, too. I guess you could say I'm interested. *Was* interested, I mean. I mean . . ." She paused. "Never mind."

"That's exactly what I was going to say," Dana told her. "Never mind Joel. It's just not worth it, when he's so . . . so. . . . Listen, take my advice. Just stay away from him."

Livvie was surprised by how forceful Dana sounded. But remembering the icy coldness of Joel's voice, she decided she didn't have much choice.

Chapter 12

Kevin's good behavior toward Livvie didn't last. The minute she and Dana set foot on the beach that evening and started walking toward the other kids, Livvie caught him watching her, his lips curling in what he must have thought was a sexy grin. Dana's head was bent; she was checking her duffel bag to make sure she'd brought a certain cassette, so she didn't notice. But Livvie had the feeling Kevin wouldn't have cared even if she did.

For a minute, she was tempted to turn around and go back to the house. But it wasn't exactly a sanctuary, not with Richardson and Joel and Kyle in it. Her mother and Joanne were visiting another high school friend, and Livvie almost wished she'd gone with them.

Looking up from her bag, Dana nudged Livvie in the side. "There's Lloyd. I told you he liked you," she said. "Why don't you hang out with him?"

"Not a bad idea," Livvie said. If she stuck with Lloyd, maybe Kevin would get the message that she wasn't interested. Not that she was interested in Lloyd, either, but he seemed like a nice, friendly guy, not a conceited jerk like Kevin.

"Kev and I'll probably leave early," Dana said with a significant smile. "So if this breaks up and I'm not here, don't wait around for me." She dropped the duffel bag and ran the rest of the way to Kevin, who lifted her off her feet and hugged her.

But all the time he was eyeing Livvie over Dana's shoulder.

Livvie picked up the bag and made a beeline for Lloyd.

She was right about Lloyd — he was a nice, friendly guy. He wasn't somebody she was going to fall madly in love with, but she wasn't expecting that. He wasn't much of a talker, so Livvie did enough talking for both of them, jabbering away about everything she could think of until her mouth was dry. The point was to keep his attention, and to keep Kevin away from her.

By the time she'd eaten two hot dogs and a

stickful of charred marshmallows, Livvie decided the plan was working. On the other side of the fire, Kevin and Dana were sticking to each other like glue, whispering and laughing at private jokes and not joining much in the general conversation. Livvie relaxed and decided it was safe to shut up for a while.

The minute Livvie got quiet, David and Sherry started talking to Lloyd about some research paper they were all supposed to be doing over vacation. Livvie listened a while, but then her mind started wandering, and it didn't take long for it to wander to Allen Richardson.

She'd just about convinced herself that the click she'd heard on the telephone wasn't him. If he was Adam Clinton, then he would have to be a master at covering up his real feelings. Still, wouldn't she have noticed more of a change in him if he thought she suspected him? If he was a murderer, and he thought *anyone* suspected him — especially his stepdaughter — he'd have to be scared. And scared people just didn't act the way Richardson did. He couldn't get any more laid back or he'd be comatose.

If only she could feel *sure* he wasn't Clinton. But she wouldn't be sure until she heard from the newspaper, or called Chesterfield.

A blast of music from the boom box jolted

Livvie back to the present. A few of the kids were dancing now. David and Sherry and Lloyd were arguing about rock groups. Dana and Kevin were still locked together. Still thinking about her stepfather, Livvie got up and walked away from the fire, down to the edge of the lake.

Before she and Dana had left the house, Livvie had heard Richardson talking about having to go home again in a couple of days. Something about a closing he had to attend. The minute he left, she'd call Chesterfield. And the newspaper articles had to have come by now. But there'd been nothing in the mail from Marta. Livvie should call her again.

A wind was coming up, and the dark water started rippling closer to the shore, lapping at the toes of Livvie's sneakers. She stepped back and walked farther on. She couldn't help wondering if Marta was just sitting on the newspaper stuff, hoping Livvie would come to her senses and forget about it.

As soon as Richardson went home, or just went to the store, as soon as she was sure he was out of the house, Livvie would call Marta again. There *had* to be something in those newspaper stories on the murder that would clear everything up.

"So there you are," a deep voice behind her

said. "I was wondering where you'd disappeared to."

It was Kevin. Livvie should have known he'd show up as soon as she let her guard down. She looked past him toward the fire. "Where's Dana?"

He chuckled softly and shook his head. "Hey, I came all the way over here just to find you. Can't you say hi?"

"Hi," Livvie said. "Where's Dana?"

Another chuckle. "She went to my car to get some more tapes," he said. "She's a big girl, don't worry about her. She can find her way back okay."

"I'm sure she can," Livvie said. "I think I'll go back to the fire now. It's getting cold out here."

Wrong thing to say.

Kevin grinned as if she'd given him an invitation, and took a step closer to her.

Livvie stepped aside.

"Hey, come on," he said. "I won't bite."

"Well, I might," Livvie said. "Listen, I'm really getting tired of this, okay?"

An innocent look. "Tired of what? Of being cold?"

Livvie just shook her head, hoping she looked the way she felt, which was disgusted.

She started to walk away, but Kevin reached out and held her arm.

Livvie stopped and faced him. He was still holding her arm, and she was about to tell him to get lost when Dana walked up, her hands full of cassette tapes. "I can't believe this," she said. She was looking at Livvie, not at Kevin.

Naturally, Kevin dropped Livvie's arm and suddenly went mute.

But he looked amused, not embarrassed.

Dana glared at Livvie a few seconds longer, then she dropped the tapes at her feet, turned around and ran off, heading for the concrete steps.

"Don't worry about it," Kevin said.

Livvie felt like hauling off and slugging him, but she ran after Dana instead.

She caught up to her at the bottom of the steps. "Dana, listen," she said, panting a little. "I know what you're thinking, but — "

"Oh, please, don't even bother," Dana said coldly. "If you're going to say you weren't coming on to Kevin, you're wasting your breath. I'm not blind, you know." There were tears in her eyes and she wiped them furiously with the back of her hand. "I'm not stupid, either. I know Kevin likes to flirt, I've seen him do it. But he wouldn't keep it up if he didn't think he could get anywhere. It's obvious you made him think he could."

Livvie shook her head. "Dana, I'm sorry, but — " She was going to say it just wasn't true, but Dana didn't give her the chance.

"Yeah, I'll bet you're sorry," she said bitterly. "You must be real sorry I came along when I did." She leaned close to Livvie and narrowed her eyes. "Why don't you just go back where you came from?" she hissed angrily. "All you do is make trouble. Nobody wants you here."

Tossing back her blonde hair, Dana turned and ran up the steps.

Livvie stood there for a moment, feeling like she'd been punched. Three out of three, she thought.

Finally, Livvie made herself walk slowly back to the fire and get the two duffel bags she and Dana had brought. Lloyd and most of the others seemed oblivious of the situation, thank goodness. But Sherry gave her a disgusted look and shook her head, as if the whole thing had been Livvie's fault.

Kevin, she noticed, was busy with the tapes Dana had dropped, wiping them on the sleeve of his sweatshirt and muttering to himself about dirt and sand. Livvie hoped they were ruined.

Without saying good-bye, Livvie left the group and started trudging up the steep steps. She wished she could take Dana's advice and go home. She was old enough to stay alone. Or she could stay with Marta, if her mother insisted.

But going home would create all kinds of problems. Her mother would want to know why, and Livvie would have to think up a good story, but the truth would probably come out. Then her mother would get all worried that she couldn't get along with anyone and needed more therapy. Joanne might get mad at her kids, which wouldn't make them like Livvie any better. Richardson, she was sure, would say something sickeningly wise and everyone would want to nominate him for stepdad of the year.

No, going home was more trouble than it was worth. She'd try to stick it out at the Wards'. Maybe by tomorrow, Dana would have cooled down enough to listen to her. It was probably a waste of time trying to reason with Kyle. But she thought there might be a chance to patch things up with Joel — *if* she could catch him in one of his good moods.

It was going to be an awful lot of work, considering none of it had been her fault, Livvie thought, puffing her way up in the dark. She was starting to get mad. She was starting to think of all the things she could have said to Kyle and Dana and Joel. Really withering comebacks, the kind she only managed in her imagination.

Stumbling on a cracked step, Livvie fell forward, bumping her knee so hard it brought tears to her eyes. She gritted her teeth and gasped, waiting for the pain to go away. Finally it did. Her eyes dry again, she took a deep breath and looked up.

Someone was waiting in the shadows at the top of the steps.

Chapter 13

Livvie felt her heart speed up and her knees go weak. She didn't move. Neither did the person in the shadows. Whoever it was, they weren't coming down the steps, or passing by. They were just waiting.

Waiting for her.

Kyle, maybe. He'd practically promised to make trouble for her. This might be what he meant. He was just the kind to hang out and try to scare her.

Or it could be Kevin. Livvie could just imagine him coming up to intercept her. Not believing she wasn't interested in him.

Slowly, Livvie looked behind her. She was much closer to the top than the bottom. If she turned and ran back down, she was sure she'd fall.

Trying not to make a sound, Livvie climbed up a step. Then she waited.

The figure still didn't move away.

Livvie took another silent step up. She was so scared her knees were still shaky. But the thought of Kyle or Kevin doing this to her made her furious.

She was almost at the top now. Frightened and angry, she dropped one of the duffel bags, got a good grip on the handles of the other one and swung it as hard as she could, aiming for the person's head. She screamed at the same time, her voice high and loud and full of fury.

"Hey, Olivia, take it easy!" Joel said. "I'm a peaceful, law-abiding citizen. I didn't come out here to get my head bashed." He moved closer and peered at her. "That is you, isn't it, Olivia?"

"Yes, it's me!" Livvie shouted. "And if you didn't want to get your head bashed, what were you doing up here lurking in the shadows like a mugger? Geez!"

"Sorry. Really, I'm sorry. Who'd you think I was, anyway?"

"I didn't really know who you were!" Livvie yelled. "You scared me to death!"

"Sorry," Joel said again. He rubbed his head and winced. "What's in that bag, anyway, bricks?"

"I wish," Livvie said. She was so mad and so relieved, her hands were shaking. "Tapes," she told him. "Dana's tapes are in the bag."

"And you're her packhorse?" Joel asked. "I saw her walking home a few minutes ago, but she didn't see me. How come you're carrying her stuff?"

"Because she — never mind," Livvie said. She picked up the other bag and took a deep breath. "You scared me. That was a really dumb thing to do, stand up here like some kind of — "

"Mugger, right." Joel stuffed his hands in his pockets and tried to smile. "There's never been a mugging in Cliffside," he informed her. "A couple of armed robberies, yes, but never — "

"Just shut up, will you?" Livvie said. "It's not funny. I can see you're in a good mood — *for now* — but I'm not."

"For now? I'm in a good mood *for now?*" Joel scratched his head and thought a minute. "Ah-ha. Dana's been trying out her theory on you, hasn't she? Her theory about how I'm going over the edge?"

"It's nothing to joke about," Livvie said.

"I'm not joking."

Livvie didn't answer. She got a better grip on the bags and started walking. Joel fell in step beside her and they walked in silence for a while. Finally, Joel said, "Don't you want to know why I was lurking up there in the shadows?"

"Not really."

"I knew you'd gone to the lake," Joel went on, as if she'd said yes, "and I wanted to come down and talk to you. See, I thought a lot about what happened this afternoon — you remember, don't you? The guitar?"

"I remember, all right."

"And I thought I'd come find you and accept your apology."

"Oh, great," Livvie said sarcastically. "I'll be able to sleep tonight without worrying about it. You don't have any idea how much better I feel."

"Wait a minute, you didn't let me finish," Joel said.

"You mean there's more? I can't wait."

"Livvie." Joel stopped walking and put his hand on her arm. Livvie stood still and looked at him. "I didn't mean that the way it sounded, about accepting your apology," he said. "I was trying to work my way up to apologizing to *you*. I acted like a complete jerk about the guitar, and I'm sorry."

Livvie looked at him for a moment longer, and then shook her head. The anger was gone and now she just felt tired. "It's all right," she said. "I'm glad you came down to find me and say that. Let's forget about it, okay?"

Joel smiled and nodded, and took one of the

bags from her. They walked on together, crossing Main Street and starting up one of the winding roads at the bottom of the hill.

After a moment, Joel said, "The guitar was my father's. It's dumb — I guess I put it on the wall so every time I looked at it, I'd remember to stay mad at him. I'm furious with him for leaving us, but I miss him, too. Does that make any sense, or is Dana right? Am I going off the deep end? She did talk to you about me, didn't she?"

"Yes," Livvie said. "She doesn't understand why you blow hot and cold, that's the way she described it. But I don't think there's anything crazy about the way you feel." She laughed a little. "I know what I'm talking about, too. I have lots of experience with people thinking *I'm* crazy."

Joel gave her a curious glance, and Livvie went on to describe how she'd felt after her father died and how she'd wound up in a hospital. "Your way is much better than mine," she said. "I should have hung something on my wall instead of falling apart. I'm not making fun of it," she added quickly, reaching out and lightly touching his arm. "I know it's important. I'm not very good at talking about things like this."

"I think you are." Joel smiled and took her

hand, and as they kept walking, he didn't let go of it.

Holding his hand, Livvie realized again how attracted she was to him. She felt a surge of warmth and closeness and for a moment, she had an almost overwhelming urge to tell him about Richardson. Joel wouldn't laugh at her, she thought, he wouldn't think she was crazy, he might even help her out. Except for Marta, Livvie had kept her suspicions about her stepfather to herself. And Marta thought she was being ridiculous. To tell somebody who'd be sympathetic would feel wonderful. Almost as wonderful as holding his hand.

But. How well did she know Joel, really? How much could she trust him? She'd made him mad once, through no fault of her own. If she told him about Richardson and then did something that made Joel freeze up again, how could she be sure he wouldn't decide to tell his mother, or hers, or Richardson himself?

She couldn't be sure, Livvie decided. She had to keep the secret about her stepfather to herself.

Joel dropped her hand then, but only so he could put his arm around her shoulder. As they walked together toward the house, Livvie moved closer to him and wrapped her free arm around his waist. She ignored the urge to tell him about Richardson and just enjoyed being with him. It was enough, for now.

Livvie didn't know what to expect when they reached the Ward house. Joel hadn't made any move to kiss her during the walk back. Of course, she hadn't made any move, either. Maybe he was waiting for her. As they climbed the front steps, she did a quick question and answer session with herself, trying to decide if she was ready to kiss him. By the time she'd decided she was, the moment was lost. The front porch light snapped on and the red door was pulled open and Livvie's mother was standing there, looking worried.

"There you are," she said. "Dana's in her room. She's been back for an hour and Kyle and Allen are in the kitchen discussing motorcycles. Joanne and I were getting worried about you two." She laughed. "But I see you're fine."

"Yep. We're fine," Livvie said. She and Joel weren't touching anymore, and she felt disappointed.

"We took the scenic route," Joel added as they walked inside. "It's slower, but the view's much better." He grinned at Livvie. "I'm thirsty. How about you?"

Livvie heard Kyle's and Richardson's voices from the kitchen and decided not to ruin the rest of the night. "I think I'll go upstairs for a while," she said. "If I don't see you later, I'll see you tomorrow. 'Night. 'Night, Mom."

With a smile, Livvie left the two of them and headed upstairs. As she reached the second floor, she thought about going to Dana's room and trying to talk to her, but she decided it was probably too soon. Give her the rest of the night to cool off, she thought. She walked past Dana's closed door to the back stairway and on up to her room.

Flicking on the light, Livvie shut the door and went straight to the bed. She wanted to lie down. But before she did, she noticed something: the bedspread was perfectly smooth, without a single wrinkle anywhere. Livvie had made the bed that morning, but had she smoothed it out that much?

Normally, a few missing wrinkles wouldn't matter, but they mattered now.

They mattered because of what she kept hidden underneath the mattress of that nicely made bed.

Her notebook about her stepfather.

Not sure whether she was imagining things, Livvie threw the side of the spread up. Then she felt along the edge of the mattress until she came to the handle. That was where she always slid the notebook, right under the handle, not so she'd remember where it was, but so she'd know if it had been moved.

Holding her breath, Livvie slid her fingers under the mattress, feeling for the spiral edge of the notebook. The notebook was there, right where it was supposed to be, centered under the mattress handle.

But its spiral edge was facing in, toward the center of the bed.

Livvie pulled the orange notebook out and sat back on her heels, looking at it and thinking.

She always slid it under so the spiral edge faced out.

At least she *thought* she always did. Maybe she'd just forgotten last night and stuck it in the other way.

Or maybe, she thought, her heart starting to race, someone had been in here, searching her room. Maybe someone else had opened it, as she was doing now. Maybe someone else had read everything she'd written down about a man named Adam Clinton, who was a murderer, and a man named Allen Richardson, who might be the same person.

Chapter 14

Livvie told herself not to panic. She couldn't be sure. She might have put the notebook back the other way. People were always insisting they'd done something or said something and then it turned out they hadn't.

Closing her eyes, she tried to remember every detail: just before she'd turned out the light last night, she'd taken the notebook out and read her notes. She remembered feeling annoyed that the stuff from the newspaper hadn't come yet. She'd wondered when it would be safe to call Chesterfield. She'd tried to think of a story to tell the high school, that's right, and she'd decided to make up something about a class reunion. Before she'd worked out all the details, she'd started to get sleepy, so she turned off the light . . . no, she'd put the notebook back first, then turned off the light. Or had she?

Which was it? Had she turned out the light first? Had she put the notebook back spiral edge out or in? Livvie couldn't remember. Maybe she was scaring herself for nothing.

She shook her head and told herself to stop thinking about it. But her brain ignored the order and went right on, trying to figure out who might have been in her room.

It could have been Kyle. Or Dana. It could even have been Joel. Holding hands with him didn't make Livvie a mindreader. For all she knew, he could have gone through her room and then been really nice to her on the way back from the lake just so she wouldn't suspect him.

She almost wished it were Joel. Or Dana or Kyle. They'd all had the time.

But then, so had her stepfather.

The thought that Richardson might have stood on this very spot and read the notes she'd written about him terrified her.

After a moment, Livvie stuck the notebook in the back pocket of her jeans and stared around the room. Nothing else seemed different. If Richardson had been there, he couldn't have been *looking* for the notebook. He didn't know it existed.

Or did he?

Livvie's mind flashed back to that scene with

Kyle. Kyle stood there, threatening her, and she'd gotten off the bed to face him. The phone book had been on the bed, and she'd been copying down area codes. When she got up, she'd kept the notebook in her hand. Kyle must have seen it. Richardson must have, too, when he came to the door.

Still feeling sick and scared, Livvie shut her eyes again and tried to remember if her stepfather had looked at her hands. Even if he had, would he have been able to read it? Had she closed the notebook when she got off the bed? She didn't know. She couldn't remember. She was making herself crazy trying.

"Livvie?" It was her mother, calling from the bottom of the stairway. "Honey, are you up there?"

Glad for the interruption, Livvie went to the door and pulled it open. "Yes, I'm up here," she called. Her voice sounded funny to her. She swallowed. "What is it?"

"We're all having popcorn in the kitchen," her mother yelled. "Come on down and join us."

All? Livvie thought. Somehow she couldn't picture Kyle sitting at the kitchen table, being chummy and sharing popcorn and jokes. Or Dana either, not that night, anyway. Richardson would be there, naturally, scoring points for being such a great guy. The whole gathering had probably been his idea.

"Livvie?"

Pretend, Livvie decided. She had to pretend nothing was wrong. For all she knew, nothing was. And she couldn't hide out up here or her mother would make a big deal out of it. She looked around her room again, trying to find a new place to put the notebook.

"Livvie! Hurry up or it'll all be gone before you get any."

"Okay, I'm coming!" The notebook could stay in her pocket for now, Livvie decided. At least she'd know it was safe.

Tucking the notebook down as deep as it would go, Livvie turned off the light and left her room, heading for the back stairway.

But as she reached the top stair, the toe of her shoe caught on the edge of the carpeting, which had come loose. Feeling herself starting to fall, Livvie reached out and grabbed hold of the banister. It made a splintering sound, sort of like a walnut being crunched in a nutcracker, only much louder.

Off balance, Livvie couldn't catch herself. As the wooden railing cracked completely, she tumbled down the narrow stairway, falling, falling. She didn't stop until she'd hit the bottom.

Chapter 15

Slightly dazed, Livvie lay on her side, waiting for her head to clear. She'd bumped it going down, and scraped her cheek on the scratchy carpeting. She was slowly sitting up when she heard a bunch of voices at the bottom of the main staircase.

"What on earth was that, Livvie?" her mother called out.

"That was me," Livvie said. "I fell."

Footsteps. Then her mother and Richardson appeared, followed by the Ward family — all four of them. Livvie stood up as her mother and Joanne buzzed around, making worried noises. "I'm okay," she said. "But the banister isn't. It broke."

Kyle made a sound, somewhere between a snort and a snicker. Dana ate a piece of popcorn. Joel raised his eyebrows at Livvie, as if to ask was she okay. Livvie nodded.

Richardson stared at Livvie, not saying anything. Then he went up the stairs to inspect the banister. In a few moments, he came back down, shaking his head. He was carrying a large, jagged splinter that had broken off from the railing. "I knew that thing was old the first time we went through the house," he said. "Not only that, but it was starting to pull away from the wall."

Livvie couldn't remember. Had it been loose? Loose enough to break like that?

She didn't think so. She was sure she would have remembered.

She hadn't pulled on it, either. Not until just a few minutes ago. It hadn't gotten so loose by itself. The carpeting at the top, where she'd caught her foot, had that been loose, too? It seemed like a strange coincidence.

Or had both been loosened deliberately?

"I feel bad, but at least you're not hurt," Richardson said. "I'll take care of it tomorrow."

"Allen, you're a godsend," Joanne said. "Everybody be careful going up and down until it's fixed, especially you, Livvie."

Livvie nodded, her eyes on the splintered piece of wood in Richardson's hands. It was big, about half a foot long, jagged along one edge and tapering to a sharp point. The way her stepfather was holding it, it reminded Livvie of a knife.

The pounding was constant.

Livvie couldn't shut it out. At first she thought it was somebody chopping wood, but now it sounded different. It was louder and closer now.

Livvie felt her heart speed up, thudding along with the pounding.

Something was beating at the door, beating at it so hard the walls were shaking. The door couldn't hold up; it would crack and buckle and then whatever was out there would break through, splintering the wood into jagged, deadly knives, and it would use those knives on Livvie.

She had to get out, but the pounding was so loud she couldn't think. Her breath came in gasps as the pounding shook the walls and the door shuddered violently.

With a final gasp, Livvie sat straight up in bed, her arms stretched out, ready to push the monstrous intruder away.

But her hands pushed only against the air. There was no monster, and the doors and walls were solid and still. There was only the pounding. As Livvie waited for her breathing to get back to normal, she realized what it was: Richardson, fixing the banister. Livvie had worked it all into a dream.

It was morning. Sunlight seeped in around the edges of the windowshades. Livvie got up and raised one of them, and the gray cat, which had been patroling the patio wall, looked up at the sudden movement. Richardson pounded especially loud just then, and the cat flicked its ears and marched away as if annoyed.

Livvie felt the same way. Couldn't Richardson have waited until she was awake to play Mr. Fixit? Yawning, she pulled on jeans and a T-shirt, stuck her feet into her moccasins and then got her notebook. She'd kept it in bed with her last night, not just under the pillow, but tucked inside the pillowcase. Now she put it back in her jeans' pocket, which was where she'd decided to keep it from now on.

Grabbing the little bag that she kept her toothbrush and stuff in, she opened the door and went into the hall.

Richardson was on the landing, his back to her. Kyle was halfway down the stairs. Kyle saw Livvie first.

She watched his expression change from a frown of concentration to a taunting smile. She looked away.

Now Richardson had seen her. "Morning,

Livvie," he said. "I'll bet we woke you up. Sorry about that, but I may have to go back home this afternoon and I wanted to get this taken care of."

"It's okay." Good, Livvie thought. Let him go back home so she could call Chesterfield. She started down the stairs, picking her way carefully between some screwdrivers and a couple of big bolts.

"Watch your step," Richardson called after her.

When she got down to Kyle, he didn't budge.

He just looked at her, as if daring her to try to get past him. Livvie looked back for a second, then stuck out her foot and used it to nudge a coffee can full of screws and nails closer to the edge of a step. The can rattled, and Kyle reacted automatically, shifting his weight to stop the can from tipping over. Livvie went on down the stairs.

A few minutes later, Livvie went into the kitchen. Dana was at the table, buttering a muffin and looking gloomy. When Livvie came in, the look changed to icy anger. Dana went on buttering the muffin, her eyes following Livvie as she went to the refrigerator. "Aren't you packed yet?" she asked.

Livvie pulled out the orange juice and poured herself a glass. "Dana . . ."

"I think you ought to get going, don't you?" Dana went on. "It's already ten. If you wait much longer, you might hit lots of traffic."

"Dana, I'm not going anywhere." Livvie took a sip of juice.

"Well, I don't see why not," Dana said. "You can drive. You don't have to wait until your mother and stepfather go. Actually, I don't even care if they stay. They're nice. It's *you* I want out of here." She took a big bite of the muffin.

Livvie put the glass down and crossed her arms. "I was hoping we could talk, so I could explain what happened. Can't you stop being mad for a second and listen?"

Dana chewed slowly, as if she was thinking it over.

Then she shook her head. "I don't want to talk, Livvie. I want you to leave. I don't know why you'd want to hang around, anyway. It can't be fun for you when nobody likes you. That includes Joel, by the way," she added. "Mom told me how you two came in together last night. You work fast, don't you?"

Livvie sighed. This was hopeless.

"But if you think he likes you, you must be as crazy as he is," Dana said. She shot her chair back and stood up. "So if you're going to stay, you'd better watch out for Joel," she said.

"You'd better watch out for all of us."

She went to the door, but before she left, she turned back. "You were lucky last night, Livvie. Next time, you might not be."

Dana left then, and Livvie picked up her juice, wondering what she was talking about.

Then it hit her — the banister. That's how she'd been lucky. Did Dana really mean that someone had fixed it so the banister would break? That's what Livvie had wondered last night. By the time she'd gone to sleep, she'd decided it wasn't true.

Now she started wondering all over again.

Kyle might have done it, she guessed. But not Joel, she couldn't believe that. And she really couldn't see Dana up there with a saw or pliers or whatever. Dana was just taking advantage of the situation to threaten her and make her nervous. She was being crazy. Nobody did it.

Then an image came back to her: Richardson, standing on the stairs with the knifelike splinter of wood in his hand. Saying that he'd known the banister was old and loose, he'd noticed it right from the beginning.

Maybe he'd made it even looser.

But why? Why, unless . . .

Livvie put the juice down slowly. Unless he *had* been in her room and seen the notebook.

Then he might fix the banister so it would break and Livvie would . . . what? Get hurt? That wouldn't do him any good.

If he really wanted to keep her quiet, he'd have to kill her.

But that fall wouldn't have killed anybody. No, this was crazy thinking.

Livvie finally finished her juice, ate a bowl of cereal and left the kitchen. She could still hear Kyle and her stepfather working away on the railing. It looked like Richardson didn't have to leave after all. Okay, so she'd call Marta anyway and talk in code or something. The newspaper articles had to have come by now.

As she crossed the back hall, Livvie noticed the door leading down into the basement was open. Looking in, she saw Joel making his way down the rickety stairs. "Hi," she said.

He stopped and looked back. Now she noticed that he was carrying a roll of wide black tape. "Olivia. Hi."

"What are you doing?"

"Your stepfather said he was going to wrap a couple of pipes down here, but Mom decided I should do it." He looked down at the roll of tape on his hand and frowned, as if he couldn't remember how it got there.

He was acting kind of funny, Livvie thought. Not unhappy or mad, just kind of remote.

"Well, when you're finished, maybe we can go to the lake or something," she said.

Joel kept staring at the tape.

"Hey, are you all right?" Livvie asked.

Joel looked at her and frowned. "Do I look sick?"

Livvie shook her head. What was the matter with him this time? "No, but you got so quiet," she explained. "I just wondered if you were okay."

He stared at her a second longer. Then he said, "I'm fine. How about you? *I* should be asking if you're all right."

"What do you mean?"

"I mean your big fall last night. You couldn't have forgotten already." Joel's serious expression shifted into a smile. But it wasn't a sympathetic one. He seemed privately amused at something. Livvie didn't know what.

"No," she said. "I haven't forgotten. And I'm okay."

"Well . . . good." Joel started to say something. But then he turned away. "Better get back to it," he murmured, going down the steps.

Livvie watched until he disappeared into the inky darkness of the basement. Hot and cold, she thought. She couldn't figure him out.

Maybe she shouldn't bother anymore.

Leaving the hall, Livvie went through the big den and around until she came to the living room. She listened a moment until she heard hammering from upstairs. Then she picked up the phone and dialed Marta's number. Marta's mother answered.

"Oh, Livvie, you just missed her," Mrs. Ryland said. "She went to the mall, and you know what that means — time and money. Do you want to leave a message?"

"I'm not sure," Livvie said. "She didn't happen to say anything about going to the post office, did she? To mail something to me?"

"As a matter of fact, she did mention that, last night," Marta's mother said. "But I saw the envelope in her room this morning after she left, so I guess she forgot it."

"Oh." Livvie wanted to ask Mrs. Ryland to rip it open and read it all to her, but that was impossible. "Well, could you please tell her that it's really important? I'm going to be here for almost another week and I need it. It's really important," she said again.

"I'll tell her the minute she gets home," Mrs. Ryland promised. "How are you, Livvie? Are you having a good time?"

"I'm fine," Livvie said. "It's nice here. Real

pretty." That ought to cover it, she thought. "Thanks, Mrs. Ryland. And you won't forget? About the envelope?"

"It's branded on my brain, don't worry."

Livvie thanked her again and they said good-bye. Good, she thought, the envelope was there. If Marta mailed it tomorrow, she'd have it in a day or two at the most. Maybe she'd even mail it today.

Livvie stood next to the phone for a moment, wondering what to do next. She didn't want to go upstairs, not with Kyle and Richardson there, and she had the feeling Dana wouldn't be asking her to the lake today. Then she remembered Joel. Down in the basement wrapping pipes.

She didn't really want to give up on him, she realized. Maybe if she went down there, she could find out what was bothering him.

She went back to the kitchen and got two cans of iced tea. She'd even let him have both if he didn't try to talk her into helping with the pipes. As she walked toward the basement door, she could still hear the pounding from upstairs. Good. Richardson couldn't have heard her talking to Marta's mother. Now if Marta would just remember to put it all in a different envelope, he'd never know what was going on.

The basement stairs were old and rickety,

with no railing. Livvie tucked both iced tea cans under one arm, and used her other hand to steady herself against the dingy brick wall. She could feel little pieces of brick flaking off under her fingers as she went down. The light from the bare bulb at the top of the steps didn't reach to the bottom, and when Livvie finally got there, she stepped into a pool of darkness.

"Joel? You still down here?" He didn't answer exactly, but Livvie heard a kind of grunt somewhere to the left. She started walking that way, and as she did, the darkness faded a bit. Daylight was making its way through one of the cloudy basement windows, just enough to keep her from bumping into anything. It didn't light up the cobwebs, though, and she shuddered as the slender threads kept brushing her face and hair.

"Joel?" she called again. Another sound, a soft thump. "Where are you, anyway?"

She kept walking slowly, expecting to see him any second. But she didn't. By now she'd passed the window and its faint light, and was in darkness again. She stopped, deciding to give it one more try. "I brought some iced tea," she said loudly. "But if you want it, you'll have to come get it. I'm not moving another inch. Just follow the sound of my voice."

Silence.

Livvie took a deep breath of the damp, musty air and shivered. Time to go back, she thought. Whatever sound she'd heard wasn't Joel.

She didn't want to stick around to find out exactly what it was.

Using the window as her guide, she headed back to the steps and the inky blackness at the bottom. She tried not to hurry, but she was starting to get spooked, so by the time she found the stairs again, she was almost running.

At the bottom of the steps, she stopped and looked up. The bulb at the top was dark. The door was closed, just a thin sliver of light seeping under it.

Livvie was still staring at that sliver of light when she heard the sound coming from behind her.

Chapter 16

Forcing down a scream, Livvie jerked around and tried to see what had made the noise.

All she saw was darkness, and far off, where the window was, some gray shadows. She got a better grip on the tea cans, felt behind her with her foot, and slowly backed up onto the bottom step. She was afraid to turn her back on whatever in the blackness had made the sound.

Backing up step by step, Livvie made her way to the top of the stairs, using her free hand for balance on the flaking brick wall. When she got to the top step, she finally turned around, found the doorknob, twisted it, and pushed.

The door didn't open.

Livvie pushed again, harder, but it still wouldn't open. Slapping her hand on the door, she called out, "Hey! Somebody come open the door, I got shut in!" She waited for a few moments, listening for footsteps.

None came.

She made a fist this time and banged on the door as hard as she could. Then she used the tea cans to hit with. She would have kicked, too, but she was afraid of losing her balance. After at least half a minute of pounding and shouting, she stopped and listened again.

Nothing.

Livvie slid her hand along the wall, trying to find a light switch, but there didn't seem to be one. It must be out in the hall. Or maybe you pulled the bulb on and off with a string. She waved her hand around in the air, but felt nothing except more cobwebs.

Where was everybody? Who'd turned off the light and shut the door? It must have been obvious that somebody was down here. You didn't just shut a door, especially to this dungeon, without checking to make sure no one was there.

Suddenly, Livvie remembered. There was a bolt on the outside of the door, near the top. She could picture it clearly.

The door wasn't just shut, it was locked. Someone had turned off the light and bolted the door.

Somebody did it on purpose.

Livvie went cold at the thought. Someone must have seen her going down, or heard her calling for Joel, and then locked her down there.

Sitting in the darkness, she shivered again. She hated the darkness. It felt like it was closing in on her. She wanted to scream again, but there was no one to hear her.

Who? Who would do this to her? Maybe Dana. After all, she'd told Livvie to watch out. So had Kyle. But Kyle was upstairs, or had been. She'd heard the hammering.

Joel? Joel hadn't made any threats. But when she'd spoken to him before, he'd been so strange. She remembered his funny smile when he asked her if she was all right. Deep down, was he still mad at her? Would that make him do something like this? Shut her up in a damp, dark basement with no way to get out?

No way to get out.

Livvie felt another scream rising in her throat. She braced herself on the crumbling brick wall and bit her lip to keep the scream down. But the thought stayed with her — someone was out to scare her, maybe even hurt her. And in spite of Dana and Kyle, and possibly even Joel, the person who'd want to hurt her the most was her stepfather.

If he thought she suspected him.

If he really was a murderer.

Richardson had been upstairs with Kyle, though. No, wait. Just because she'd heard hammering didn't mean they were both up there. One of them could have come down and seen her go into the basement. It could have been Kyle.

But it could have been Richardson.

Crazy, Livvie told herself. She was thinking crazy again. She forced the thoughts away and pounded on the door again, then turned around and sat on the top step to wait. Somebody would have to come eventually. Not everyone in this house was her enemy.

Livvie had forgotten about the sound that had frightened her before, but now she heard it again. A kind of swishing sound, like cloth rubbing against something. Her heart had almost settled down, but now it started racing again. She stood up, her legs quivering, ready to run. Run where?

There was nowhere to go.

Then she heard a faint thump, followed by another and another. It was on the stairs.

Livvie felt the door at her back. She opened her mouth to scream, when something bounded the rest of the way up the steps and landed at her feet.

The cat. The gray cat she'd seen out on the

patio had gotten into the basement somehow and followed her around. Now it was rubbing against her ankles, purring like a motorboat.

Livvie let her breath out and reached down to pet the cat. "Sorry," she said. "You can't get out this way." To prove her point, she tried the door again. The door hadn't magically unbolted itself, but as Livvie kept pushing, she realized that there was some give to it. The bolt didn't keep it completely tight. If she could find a screwdriver or something like that down here, maybe she could wedge it in and push the bolt loose. Anything would be better than just sitting in the dark and waiting.

Leaving the iced tea cans at the top of the stairs, Livvie made her way down again and onto the basement floor. She hated this place. She didn't want to walk along the gritty floor and feel the blackness close around her like a heavy blanket. She couldn't breathe right. She wanted to cry.

But she had to get out. She made herself start to walk.

The cat walked along with her, weaving in and out of her legs. Slowing her down. But Livvie was glad for the company. The cat was real.

Everything else seemed like a nightmare.

When she'd come down before, she hadn't

found where Joel had been working, so she went in a different direction this time. It took her by the big furnace and underneath the snaking ducts. Livvie stopped and looked around. Where were the pipes Joel had been talking about? Pipes were on the ceiling usually, but all she could see were the silvery heating ducts, cobwebs draped around them like fine netting.

She shuddered and made herself keep walking.

After a moment, the cat bounded ahead of her and disappeared. Livvie heard a kind of scrabbling noise, then silence again. The cat must have gotten out the way it came in, probably through a crack in a wall or something. She wished it hadn't gone.

Now she was alone again.

Livvie kept walking, shivering in the cold air below ground. Her moccasins shuffling along the gritty floor made the only sound she heard except her own breathing. If she'd heard footsteps above, she'd have gone back to the stairs and pounded again, but she heard nothing from above, not even a creak. It was as if the house had suddenly been evacuated.

It seemed like hours, but it was probably less than a minute when she saw some pipes running along the ceiling. They were brown and rusty-looking, they probably hadn't been touched in years. But they looked like they kept going on into another part of the basement. Livvie followed them, hoping to find the place where Joel had been, and maybe find some kind of tool to use on the door.

Livvie wasn't sure when the darkness became almost total. It had always been dark, but her eyes had adjusted and she could see well enough to keep from running into anything. But after she'd followed the pipes for a moment, she realized she could barely see anything anymore. She stuck a hand out and felt nothing, so she crept forward cautiously, thinking she'd eventually come to another window and some more feeble light.

The darkness didn't let up. It was inky, thick, and it seemed to go on forever. Livvie decided *she* wouldn't go on forever. It was cold down here. It was airless. She couldn't breathe.

Gasping, she turned around, took three steps, and walked straight into a wall. It was crumbling, like everything else, and when Livvie pulled back, she felt something wet on her forehead. Water or blood? She wiped her head with her fingers and winced. She'd cut herself.

She must have gotten turned around somehow, right before she hit the wall. God, she was stupid to have come down here.

She put her hand on the wall as a guide and walked a little more. She wasn't sure where she was now. She couldn't see the pipes or the ducts. Her breath came faster. She was gasping, almost whimpering. But she made herself keep going.

Livvie walked on, her fingers trailing across the wall, and after a few moments, she felt the ceiling scraping her head. She hunched over and went a little farther. Her moccasins stopped making that gritty sound. The floor was softer now, with loose pebbles poking into her feet through the leather. In the dark, she hadn't noticed it, but the floor had sloped and the ceiling had lowered. Now she was in the worst part of the basement, the crawl space.

Livvie stopped, feeling dizzy and more frightened than ever. It wasn't the dirt or the darkness or the thoughts of spiders that scared her. It was the closeness of the place. She couldn't stand being shut in. She couldn't even zip herself into a sleeping bag without feeling like she was being buried alive.

She had to get out of there.

Her breathing fast and ragged, Livvie turned around and put her other hand against the wall. All she had to do was follow it back the way she'd come. Right. She took two steps and stopped again.

She'd heard something. A creak, a scraping sound. Now there was another creak. It was the stairs, footsteps on the stairs. Someone was coming down.

"Hey!" Livvie shouted. "I'm all turned around down here!"

Another creak, but no answer. Livvie was just about to shout again when she suddenly felt her face get hot as her heart sped up in fear. She'd shouted loud enough for anyone to hear her. Somebody was on the stairs. Somebody had heard her.

But they weren't answering.

The stairs creaked again.

Not caring about anything but getting away, Livvie ran. She ran blindly. She didn't bother to use the wall anymore. The ceiling scraped her head and cobwebs wrapped themselves across her face and throat. A nail caught on her T-shirt and ripped painfully across her arm. Her lungs were on fire, she couldn't get her breath. She stumbled and fell twice, scratching her palms on the rocks and dirt. A moccasin came off, and she felt wildly around the floor for it, then went on without it. She hardly felt the pebbles cutting into her bare foot.

All she thought about was getting away.

The third time Livvie tripped, she went sprawling forward on her hands and knees, scraping her palms again. But this time as she pulled herself up, she saw that she'd landed on cement, not gravel and dirt. She scrambled to her feet and was able to stand straight. The ceiling was a good foot above her head there. And up ahead, she could see the silvery glint of the heating ducts. She'd come full circle.

Her breathing slowed down, her heart slowed down, and soon she was able to listen.

Nothing.

No creaking, no scraping. Nobody breathing but her. She moved ahead more slowly now, limping a little because her foot hurt. The furnace loomed up ahead, and from there, Livvie was able to make her way back to the stairs.

The light was still off.

But the door was wide open.

Chapter 17

Everybody had an excuse.

Dana said she'd been in her room the whole time and hadn't heard a thing. Kyle and Richardson said they'd finished the banister and gone out to the garage. Joanne and Livvie's mother had been shopping for groceries. Joel had taken a break from the pipes and walked to the lake. He hadn't shut the door when he left.

"Are you sure the door was locked?" Dana asked her at dinner. She sounded sweet and sincere, but Livvie knew better. "I mean, if nobody shut it, then how could it have been locked?"

Kyle laughed. "The phantom did it."

"The wind probably blew it shut," Joel said. "There's a breeze in that hallway."

"Did the wind lock the door, too?" Kyle laughed again.

Everyone looked at Livvie, as if she could explain.

No one had been around when she'd come out of the basement, so she'd gotten cleaned up, then stayed in her room the rest of the day. She'd been scared to death, but she'd decided not to say anything. Except the cut on her forehead and a bruise on her cheek were impossible to hide. When she'd come down for dinner, there'd been all kinds of questions.

"You're having your share of adventures here, aren't you?" Dana asked. "First the banister, now the basement."

"I wouldn't call it an adventure." Livvie heard her voice rising, but she couldn't stop it. "It was awful down there!"

"I'm sure it was," her mother said. "But you're out now, Livvie. Calm down."

"I am calm!" Livvie picked up her fork and put it down again. "But everybody keeps talking about phantoms or the wind, like it was just an accident or like I imagined it. It wasn't an accident! I didn't imagine it!"

"Then it must have been Kyle's phantom," Dana said. She covered her mouth with her hand, but her eyes were sparkling with laughter.

"It wasn't a phantom," Livvie said. "I ought to know, I was down there. Somebody . . ."

"Somebody what?" Kyle asked.

Livvie hadn't told them everything. She hadn't told them about the footsteps on the stairs. Someone had been on the stairs, heard her yell, and not answered. The same someone who'd bolted the door, she was sure.

Everyone was looking at her again, waiting for her to say something. They really think I'm crazy, she thought. She felt so alone, she wanted to cry.

Glancing around the table, Livvie caught Richardson watching her. His light brown eyes were questioning, as if deeply concerned. She couldn't stand it, not from him.

She looked away. "Okay," she said, "I think Joel's probably right and the wind blew the door shut. It probably sticks." Now she looked at Richardson again. She even managed to smile at him. "Didn't you say it needed planing or something, Allen?"

Her stepfather nodded.

"That must be it, then," Livvie said. "I'll bet it stuck and I just didn't try hard enough to get it open."

No one said anything. She looked at Joel, but he was staring off into the distance, thinking about something else. Or else he just didn't want to meet her eyes.

Livvie forced a nervous laugh and forked up

some salad. "No phantom or anything," she went on. "Just me, thinking I was locked in and getting scared." She ate the salad. Let them think she was weak and hysterical. Better that than crazy.

She didn't know if it worked or not. But at least everyone finally stopped talking about what had happened to her. She could still feel them watching her, though. She helped herself to more salad and ate as if she hadn't eaten all day. Actually, she hadn't, but her stomach was in knots and she really didn't want anything.

After a few moments, her mother said, "Oh, Livvie, I almost forgot. Marta called."

"*She did?* Why didn't you get me?"

"Well, my gosh, Livvie, don't jump all over me, I didn't know where you were," her mother said. "I thought you'd probably gone to the lake with Dana. Nobody was around when Joanne and I got home."

"Okay, sorry," Livvie said. She wiped her mouth and pushed back her chair. "I'll go call her now."

"No, she said she wouldn't be at home tonight," her mother told her. "But she left a message."

Livvie felt her mouth go dry. She looked at her stepfather. He was watching her, listening.

What if the message mentioned *The Morrisville Sun*?

Without thinking, Livvie held out her hand, as if to keep her mother quiet. But it was too late.

"Let's see," Patricia said. "She said to tell you she has to be at the dentist's tomorrow at ten-thirty, and she'll go to the post office right after. Does that make sense?"

Livvie had been holding her breath. Now she let it out, but slowly, to keep her relief from showing. "Um, yes, it makes sense," she said. "I forgot to bring some notes with me. She's mailing me a copy of hers."

Livvie managed to go on eating as if the message wasn't important at all. After a minute, she looked at Richardson again. Their eyes met, and he smiled. He was wearing his glasses. His *reading* glasses, Livvie thought.

Behind them, his brown eyes were narrowed. Curious. Calculating.

Livvie looked away.

Another day or two, she thought. Another day or two and she'd have the newspaper stories.

And the answer to her questions.

The cat glared at her, its amber eyes like twin fires in the inky darkness. Livvie felt betrayed. They were basement buddies. Hadn't they been stuck down here together, just a few hours ago?

The cat stared at her a few seconds longer, then moved ahead, its gray coat melting into the shadows. Livvie followed. She had to find out how the cat had gotten out before. It was important. What if she got locked in here again? Maybe the crack in the wall would be big enough for her. Then she could get out, too.

She wasn't sure why she'd come down here now, so late, except that she had to find out. She followed the cat.

The basement looked different. There were doors that hadn't been there before. Why hadn't she seen them?

Now she heard the creaking again.

Footsteps on the stairs.

Somebody coming down after her.

Up ahead, the cat strode on, then stopped in front of a door and looked at Livvie again. As Livvie came closer, the cat flattened its ears and drew back its lips, exposing white, needle-sharp teeth. A low, gutteral sound came from its throat.

It was snarling at her.

Livvie stopped, but it was too late.

With a hiss and another snarl, the cat bunched itself and sprang out of the shadows, its claws and fangs aiming straight for Livvie's face.

Livvie threw up her hands and started to scream.

But the scream died in her throat as she came awake. She sat up and looked around, pushing her tangled hair out of her face.

Just a dream.

No wonder, she thought. Anybody who got stuck down in that dungeon was bound to have nightmares.

She pushed the dream out of her mind and lay back down, straightening the covers and bunching the pillow under her cheek. She was still groggy; maybe she could go right back to sleep. There was a lot on her mind, especially Allen Richardson, but she didn't want to lie awake thinking about him. It was better to think about him in the daylight, when her mind wasn't fuzzy. She closed her eyes and started composing a Spanish paper in her head. That almost always worked.

Livvie didn't know how much time had passed when she suddenly jerked awake again.

The room looked the same — dark. It wasn't pitch-dark, like the basement, but the sky outside the windows hadn't lightened at all. She'd probably only been asleep for a few minutes. Back to the Spanish paper.

It might have worked again, except for the noise.

It wasn't loud, but the house was so quiet Livvie could hear every little tick and creak.

This wasn't a creak, though.

It was almost like someone breathing. In and out, soft and steady.

Maybe she wasn't really awake, Livvie thought. That happened sometimes, being asleep and knowing she was dreaming. Then she'd usually wake up. Or the dream would change.

The breathing sound didn't stop.

Livvie turned from her side to her back. She felt the sheets slide against her skin. She didn't think she was dreaming anymore. She held her breath and listened.

In and out, the soft, rhythmic breathing went on.

Livvie opened her eyes. Across the room was the shadowy figure of a person, standing in the open closet door.

It was a dream, of course. All she had to do was blink, and it would go away.

Livvie blinked. She rubbed her eyes with the back of her hand.

The figure didn't go away. The breathing went on.

It was a dream. It had to be. Livvie felt

sweat beading on her forehead. Her heart throbbed in her ears. She kicked her legs, felt the sheets again. Soft. Soft and quiet, like the breathing across the room.

The figure moved. Something pale. Skin? A hand? The figure was moving. Coming toward her.

Livvie tried to yell. Her throat was dry and it was more of a gasp.

The figure moved again. It blurred and moved deeper into the closet.

It isn't a dream, Livvie thought.

She opened her mouth and shattered the silence of the house with a piercing scream.

Chapter 18

Still screaming, Livvie scooted back in the bed, grabbed the pillow and flung it at the closet, sending the wire clothes hangers into a frenzy of rattling. Then she was out of the bed and across the room, pulling open the door so hard it bounced off the wall and slammed behind her as she stumbled into the dim hallway.

"There's somebody!" she shouted breathlessly, running for the stairs, "there's somebody in my room!"

She'd only gone down two steps when Joel, followed by his mother, came tearing into sight and started climbing up to her.

"Don't come up!" Livvie shouted. "There's somebody in my room — it's not safe! Go back down!"

They stopped and waited for Livvie to reach them. By the time she had, the rest of the household had appeared.

"My God, Livvie, are you all right?" her mother asked.

"Yes, yes, come on, let's go!" Livvie said. "There's somebody in my room, don't you understand?"

Kyle yawned and nudged Joel in the side, and the two of them followed Richardson, who had already reached the top of the stairs.

"What are they doing?" Livvie asked.

"They're going to your rescue," Dana said sarcastically.

"Dana!" Joanne said. "Livvie had a scare. What's the matter with you?"

"Geez," Dana said. "I get waked up by all this shrieking and you gripe at me? I thought somebody died or something."

"Just watch your mouth," Joanne told her.

A scare. Livvie couldn't believe this. "It was more than a scare," she said. "Somebody was in my room and everybody's standing around like it happens all the time!" She was about to point out that they should maybe call the police when Richardson spoke from the top of the stairs.

"Everything's fine," he said. He tightened the belt on his navy blue bathrobe and started down. Joel and Kyle appeared behind him and came down, too.

"What do you mean, fine?" Livvie asked.

"Didn't you see the closet door? And the pillow — I threw a pillow."

"Really lethal," Kyle said, low enough so his mother couldn't hear. "I'll bet that scared him."

"We saw the closet and everything," Joel said to Livvie. He sat down on the bottom step and looked at her curiously. "But there wasn't anyone there. The closet's empty except for clothes."

"Oh, geez," Dana muttered.

"Are you sure it wasn't a dream, Livvie?" her mother asked.

"Of course I'm sure!" Livvie said. "I know when I'm dreaming. I'd already had one dream and I was trying to go back to sleep. This wasn't any dream, okay?"

"Well there's nobody in your room or your closet," Kyle said. "And there's no way anybody could get in except through the door because the windows are shut and there isn't even a drainpipe to climb up. So if it wasn't a dream, you tell us what it was."

"Wait a minute," Joanne said thoughtfully. "Just hold on a second." She closed her eyes. When she opened them again, she looked suspiciously at her three kids. "The secret passage."

"What?" Livvie asked.

Joanne nodded. "Don't you remember, I said

this house had a secret passage? Now that I've thought about it, I seem to recall that there's an opening to it in the back of the closet in that very room."

"I thought I noticed a panel or something like that when I was looking in there just now," Richardson said. "I didn't think anything about it, though."

"Well, I'm thinking about it," Joanne said, her eyes still on her kids. "Okay. I want to know who did this and I want to know now."

Livvie looked at them. Joel and Kyle were fully dressed at . . . what? She glanced at Joel's watch. At almost three in the morning. Dana had on a big black T-shirt that came to her knees. She supposed any one of them could have snuck into her room to frighten her. But all three of them were denying it, loudly.

"Mother! I can't believe you! I wouldn't go sneaking around any creepy secret passage just to scare Livvie," Dana said. "I've got much better things to do with my time."

"You know I wouldn't do something like that, Mom," Joel said. "I fell asleep reading and I didn't wake up until Livvie screamed."

Kyle raised his hands. "Don't look at me," he said. "You can pin a lot of stuff on me if you want, but forget this. I didn't do it."

They sounded pretty convincing, and seeing

the look on Joanne's face, Livvie could tell she believed them. Her mother and Richardson did, too. Great, she thought. They all think I dreamed it or made it up. It was happening again, just like the basement.

"Look, you guys can stand around all night if you want to," Kyle said. "But I'm going to finish listening to my tape and then try to get some sleep."

"Me, too," Dana said. She followed Kyle down the hall and out of sight.

"Well!" Livvie's mother said brightly. "I guess maybe we should all go back to bed. What do you think, Livvie? Will you be able to sleep all right now?"

Livvie looked at Joel, hoping to get some support from him, but he was in the middle of a jaw-cracking yawn. "Sure," she said. "I'll be fine." The others were probably expecting her to apologize for disturbing everyone, but she wasn't about to. "Good night," she said.

Back in her room, Livvie leaned against the door for a moment, waiting for her anger to die down. Then she crossed to the closet and picked up the pillow, which had been pushed to the side. Her notebook was still inside the pillowcase. She'd forgotten about it when she threw the pillow and she was glad to see it hadn't fallen out for Richardson to find.

She tossed the pillow on the bed, then pushed some clothes aside and looked at the back wall of her closet. Kyle or one of the others had left the closet light on, and she was able to see the outline of the panel Richardson had talked about. There were no hinges that she could see, and no handle. They must be on the other side. She reached out and pushed against it, to see if it would spring open, but it didn't. Running her hands up the back wall, she could feel that the panel was about as tall as she was. A person would have to bend just a little to get through. And if there was a handle on the other side, then all they'd have to do is pull it shut behind them. Simple.

Simple and scary. Livvie didn't expect anyone to try it again, but just in case, she dragged her suitcase into the closet and shoved it up against the wall.

She went to the bed and sat down, then jumped up almost immediately. She knew she wouldn't sleep, not yet, anyway. She was too mad. She was also thirsty.

Quietly, Livvie left her room and went down the stairs, her fingers trailing on the smooth wood of the new banister. As she walked toward the front landing, she heard voices, and when she reached the end of the hall, she could see that a downstairs light was on. She would have kept going on, down the other hall to the bathroom, except she heard her name mentioned. Without making a sound, she went halfway down the main staircase and listened.

"I know," Livvie's mother was saying, "but she won't talk to me about it."

"When do kids ever talk to their parents?" Joanne asked.

"She's just been so edgy," Patricia said. "Even before we came here. I was hoping the trip would help, but now I'm not sure. I know the banister really broke, but the basement? And tonight? She's acting like they were conspiracies instead of accidents."

"I'm sure things will settle down again when you get back home," Joanne said.

"I think Joanne's probably right." Richardson's voice. "Livvie's had a rough time — her father's death, getting used to our marriage. She's bound to have ups and downs. I don't think it's anything serious."

Livvie heard her mother sigh and say something else. Probably that she hoped her kid wasn't ready for an institution. She didn't stick around to hear more. She wasn't thirsty anymore, either, so she went quietly back up to her room and sat on the bed. She should have been scared to death, she knew, but she felt calm. Good, she thought, she'd have to be calm to handle what was happening.

Richardson was really a piece of work. Sticking up for her, pretending to be so understanding. When all the time, he was the one who was making her seem crazy.

Livvie was sure of it now. The banister, the basement, and the secret panel in her closet — they were all Richardson's doing. She wasn't doing any crazy thinking, she'd been right to suspect him from the first. He knew the house better than anyone, even the people who lived here. The first day they'd gotten here, he'd asked for a big tour. Joanne couldn't remember where the secret passage was then, but she'd mentioned it. And Richardson had found it.

She didn't know what had set him off. The phone call to Marta, the notebook, Marta herself? It didn't matter. What mattered was that he knew. And he was after her.

Of course, he wasn't going to kill her right off the bat. No, he was cleverer than that. He was going to make all kinds of "unexplainable" things happen to her, make her nervous and edgy.

Then, when he killed her, everybody would think she'd done it herself.

The best part of his plan was, no one would

believe her if she said anything. After all, he was the nicest guy in the world. Everyone liked and respected him, even Kyle. Richardson had even come to Livvie's defense when her own mother thought she was starting to fall apart.

When she did fall apart — according to his plan — he'd shake his head and cluck his tongue and look real sad that he'd been so wrong about her. "I guess you were right, Pat," Livvie could hear him saying. "I'm so sorry."

So sorry. Livvie shook her head, blocking out the imaginary voice. She'd been holding herself rigid, and now she was starting to shake. She wrapped her arms around herself, trying to be still. She couldn't get scared, not now. If she got scared, she wouldn't be careful. And she had to be careful, had to watch Richardson, never be alone with him, never let him see that she'd figured it out. He was setting the stage. He wouldn't kill her there and involve the Wards. No, he'd wait until they were back home and she was alone in the house.

So she was safe for now. If only there was someone she could tell about this, someone who'd believe her.

Gradually, the shaking stopped and Livvie lay down on the bed. She left the light on and stared at the door, waiting for morning.

* * *

The house was quiet when Livvie went downstairs the next day. She remembered Richardson saying something about working up on the roof today, but she didn't hear any pounding.

The kitchen was empty, and when Livvie went to the refrigerator for juice, she saw a note with her name on top. It was from her mother. She and Joanne had gone to the mall, the note said. Allen had to leave early and go home for a closing; he'd be back around one-thirty or so. Livvie was to have fun today.

Have fun. She wasn't sure about that, but as long as she had the house to herself, she could call Chesterfield. She left the kitchen and headed for the living room, pulling her notebook out of her back pocket as she went.

In the living room, she sat on the couch and pulled the phone into her lap. There were some pencils in the drawer of the end table and she took one out. The notebook was open beside her, the Iowa area codes written down. Livvie ran through her story one more time, then picked up the phone and got long-distance information.

She got lucky with the area code on the first try. The operator gave her the number she wanted, and Livvie jotted it down and hung up. Then, before she could talk herself out of it, she picked up the phone again and punched the number of Chesterfield high school.

"This is kind of complicated," she said to the woman who answered. "But my father went to your school back in the sixties and I'm trying to round up some of the friends he's mentioned, for a surprise reunion."

"How nice," the woman said.

"Yes, well, I was just wondering," Livvie said. "You wouldn't happen to have records that go back that far, would you?"

The woman laughed. "I'll bet you're from New York or some big city, honey. You think we don't have computers out here in the hinterlands."

Livvie laughed, too. "I didn't mean it that way. I just thought . . ."

"Oh, don't worry about it," the woman said. "Now, just tell me what you need to know and I'll see if I can help."

Livvie took a deep breath. "The name of my father's friend is Allen Richardson," she said. She gave the dates when Richardson would have been in the high school, then sat back and waited to hear that there was no record of an Allen Richardson.

After a few minutes, the woman came back on the line. "Well, this is a small school," she said, "so it's not as hard for us to keep track of our kids as some places, but I'm afraid — "

"He didn't go there?" Livvie asked.

"Oh, no, I have an Allen Richardson listed," the woman said. "But I don't have any address I could give you."

Livvie wasn't sure she'd heard right. She tightened her hold on the phone. "Allen Richardson went there?"

"Yes, but what I'm saying is I can't tell you anything else. You wanted an address, didn't you?" the woman asked. "So you could ask him to that reunion for your dad?"

Livvie found her voice long enough to thank the woman. Then she hung up and stared at the phone. She went over the woman's words in her mind, trying to make them come out different, but they came out the same way every time.

He went there. Allen Richardson went to Chesterfield high, just like he'd said.

Back then, though, his name wasn't Allen Richardson. It was Adam Clinton.

Unless Livvie was wrong. Oh, God, was she wrong about him? Was she crazy after all?

"Olivia?"

Livvie jerked her head up and saw Joel standing in the archway. His sunglasses were pushed down his nose, and he was looking at her curiously. "Are you okay?" he asked.

Livvie shook her head.

He looked at the phone, then back at her face. "What is it? Did . . . is somebody sick or something?"

"No." Livvie put the phone back on the table and stood up. "Nobody's sick. I just . . ." She stopped and took a shaky breath.

He crossed the room and took her hand. "Come on," he said. "Let's row out to the middle of the lake. It'll be quiet out there."

Livvie nodded and they left the house, walking to the lake without saying a word to each other. Joel didn't seem to expect any conversation, which was good, because Livvie's thoughts were so jangled that nothing she said would have made any sense.

There were only two other people at the lake, a woman and a little girl walking along the water's edge, throwing sticks for their dog.

Joel and Livvie got in a weathered rowboat, and Joel rowed them out past the aluminum platform to the center of the lake. Livvie watched the water ripple under the oars and listened to the dog bark as it raced after the sticks. She still didn't say anything.

After a while, she realized Joel wasn't rowing anymore. The boat was rocking gently, drifting a little. Joel had pulled the oars up and was watching her, chin in his hands, elbows on his knees. "You feel like telling me?" he asked. "You don't have to, I just thought you might want to. Or we could just drift around for a while and then leave. Whatever." He smiled. "You can row back."

Livvie managed to smile, too, and suddenly the need to tell someone was overwhelming.

"It's about my stepfather," she said. "I think he's a murderer."

Chapter 19

Livvie started at the beginning, from the time she'd seen Richardson's face on *Fugitives from Justice*. She told Joel everything. She tried to speak calmly, but every once in a while she'd hear her voice rising. When it did, she'd stop and wait until she could control it again.

She didn't look at Joel very often. He had his sunglasses stuck on top of his head and she was afraid of what she might see in his eyes — doubt, disbelief, maybe even laughter. She watched the dog racing into the lake, or she looked at her hands, clasping and unclasping as she talked.

"After I saw the television show, I kept telling myself I was wrong," she said. "I don't like Richardson, and I thought maybe that's why I was so ready to believe he's Adam Clinton. But I couldn't stop thinking about it. How much they look alike. Have you noticed Richardson's eyebrows?" she asked.

"You mean how they're always up?" Joel raised his own eyebrows.

"That's it," Livvie said. "And he tilts his head. And he's got this birthmark and his hand — have you seen that?"

Joel nodded.

"Well, Clinton is exactly the same — the eyebrows and everything," Livvie said. "There's other stuff, too. He said he went to high school in California, and then he talked about Iowa. And his glasses . . ." Livvie stopped and pulled the notebook out of her pocket. "Here, I wrote it down," she said, handing it to Joel.

Joel opened the notebook as Livvie went on talking. "I don't know how he found out that I suspected him," she said. "I think he must have heard me talking to Marta. Then he searched my room and found that notebook. Anyway, he knows. I'm sure he did something to the banister so it would break, and locked me in the basement, and came into my room last night."

Joel looked up from the notebook. "You don't think it was Kyle? Or Dana? I heard about what happened with Kevin," he said. "I was kind of thinking one of them was doing these things to you."

"So did I, for a while," Livvie said. "But that's what Richardson wants me to think. I'm sure of it. It was really convenient for him that they got mad at me. So he used it. But he's the one who's after me."

Joel looked at her notebook again while she told him her theory; that Richardson was trying to scare her and make everyone think she was having another breakdown, then kill her. "And people would think I committed suicide," she said. "I . . . I kind of broke down when my father died. My mother's always watching me now. She tries not to be obvious, but I know. She's afraid I'll crack up again, and Richardson knows it. It'll be easy for him to convince everybody I killed myself."

Joel looked up from the notes. "What about the phone call?" he asked. "When I came into the living room, you were holding the phone and you were real upset. That had something to do with this, didn't it?"

Livvie nodded and told him about the call to Chesterfield. She wished she didn't have to, but she could hardly leave it out. "I know what it sounds like," she said. "That I really am imagining the whole thing. I mean, he went to that high school, like he said. And if he did, he isn't Adam Clinton. But he is — I know he is."

"I guess it would be kind of a coincidence if

another Allen Richardson went there, or there were two of them," Joel said thoughtfully.

"Yes. Too much of a coincidence." Livvie looked away, toward the shore. The dog was climbing out of the lake, shaking itself and showering its owners with water. Livvie turned back to Joel. "I can't explain Chesterfield," she said. "I'm not going to try. I know I'm right. He's Adam Clinton. I knew it the minute I saw him on television, although I didn't want to believe it. He killed his wife and stepdaughter in a fire and took off and just kind of . . . started another life. It sounds impossible, but they wouldn't have a show like *Fugitives from Justice* if there weren't any fugitives. He's one of them and as soon as I get those newspaper articles from Marta, I'm sure I'll be able to prove it."

Joel handed back the notebook and they sat in silence for a moment. Then he said, "Bizarre. Really . . ." He shook his head, as if he couldn't think of another word for the situation.

"Weird. I know," Livvie said.

"No wonder you're ready to freak out — I'm sorry, I didn't mean it that way," he added quickly. "I just meant I don't blame you for being . . ."

"Edgy?" Livvie said with a little smile. "Nervous? Hysterical?"

"Yeah," he agreed. "Well, maybe not hysterical. But if I thought somebody wanted to kill me, I'd probably be in worse shape than you." He leaned forward, rocking the boat a little, and took her hand. "Hang in there, Livvie. If you think I can help, tell me."

Livvie squeezed his hand in thanks, and after a moment, he leaned back and took the oars. They were both quiet going back to shore. Livvie felt talked out and she figured Joel was probably thinking over everything she'd told him. She was sure he hadn't expected anything like this.

As they left the lake and headed back to the house, Joel finally started talking. Not about what she'd told him, but about music and movies and school, things they'd never talked about before. Livvie learned a lot about him: he ran on the cross-country team, he liked history and rap music, his favorite color was blue, he wasn't very good in Spanish either.

Livvie was interested, but she was more interested in what Joel thought about her story. He didn't bring it up again, though. On the lake, he'd been shocked, confused, sympathetic, all the things she'd expected and hoped for. He'd had all the right reactions.

But he never once said he believed her.

Livvie couldn't help wondering if it had been a mistake to tell him at all.

It was lunchtime when they got back to the house. No one else was there. Joel had some errands to do, so Livvie fixed herself a sandwich and took it up to her room to eat. When she finished, she set the plate on the floor and stretched out on her bed. She hadn't slept more than an hour or two last night, and she was asleep the minute her head hit the pillow.

She might have slept straight through the afternoon if it hadn't been for the pounding. Couldn't be the banister, she thought sleepily. Richardson already did that.

Richardson. The thought of her stepfather brought Livvie awake completely, and she sat up, her heart hammering. She couldn't believe it — she'd actually come up here and gone to sleep without putting something in front of her door to make sure she'd hear him if he came in.

Livvie got up, almost stepping on her empty sandwich plate, and pulled open the door. The hallway was empty. She shut it as tightly as she could and went back to the closet. The suitcase hadn't been disturbed.

The hammering went on, broken up by some

kind of ripping sound, and Livvie finally figured out where it was coming from. The roof. Richardson must be up there, doing some repair work.

Looking out, Livvie saw an aluminum ladder leaning against the house, a few feet to the side of her windows. The cat was on the patio wall, sunning itself. As Livvie looked, she saw Joel emerge from the back of the house, a hammer sticking through one of the loops on his jeans. He tested the ladder, then began climbing up.

Her window was open just a couple of inches, and Livvie started to raise it more, then decided not to. The noise might make Joel jump and lose his balance. He was climbing carefully, looking up, and she heard him say, "Mr. Richardson? I'm coming up. You want to hold the ladder up there?"

There was a scrabbling noise overhead, then Livvie heard Richardson say, "Got it. Come on. Did you get the crowbar?"

"Geez, no, I forgot it," Joel said. He glanced down. "Okay, I'll go . . ."

"No, no, never mind," Richardson said. "Most of these shingles are coming off pretty easily. We can get it later if we have to."

Joel kept climbing, and as he drew himself up closer to Livvie's windows, he glanced over and saw her. "Hey, Olivia!" he called. "There's a crowbar down on the kitchen table. You scared of heights?"

Livvie raised the window. "No," she said. "Do you want me to bring it up?"

"Yeah, that'd be great. I hate heights." Joel made a funny face and climbed out of Livvie's sight.

Livvie had been wondering why Joel would be helping her stepfather, after what she'd said about him. Was the funny face his way of saying he didn't have much choice?

Down in the kitchen, Livvie picked up the crowbar and went out onto the patio. The cat was still there, looking up at the roof. Livvie scratched it between the ears for a second, then went over to the ladder.

Sticking the crowbar in her belt loop, she gave the ladder a little shake, to make sure it was steady. Then she started up, the crowbar banging noisily every time she took a step. After she passed the second floor windows, she stopped and looked down. The cat was watching her, looking smaller now.

Livvie turned back to the ladder and kept going. "I'm on my way!" she called. "Joel?"

She could hear prying and ripping noises and figured they must be on another part of the roof. She kept climbing, drawing level with the windows in her room.

After about five more rungs, Livvie's eyes drew level with the gutter. It obviously hadn't been cleaned in a while; matted leaves and twigs filled it to the rim.

She went up another rung, and now the gutter was at her waist. There was only one more rung, and Livvie climbed onto it. The roof slanted steeply. It was true what she'd told Joel, that she wasn't afraid of heights, but climbing onto a steeply pitched roof was something else. She decided to just toss the crowbar up and let them come get it.

To toss the crowbar, though, she had to get it out of her belt loop. And that involved letting go of the ladder. Gingerly, Livvie let go with one hand and tried to work the crowbar out, but it kept catching on the loop.

Okay, she thought. Two hands. She leaned her weight forward and tried to unloop the crowbar without looking at it. The ladder shook with her movements, and she grabbed hold, forgetting about the crowbar.

It would be much safer to sit on the roof, get settled, and then get the crowbar out.

Slowly, Livvie eased a knee up past the gutter and onto the roof. So far so good. Then she stretched her hands up, flattened them on the roof, and pushed, bringing her other knee up and trying to twist around into a sitting position. Her knee hit the ladder and she heard the grating sound as it slid along the gutter, but she couldn't do anything about it.

It happened so fast, Livvie didn't even have time to scream.

She felt something shift under her knees, and suddenly she was sliding backwards. Her fingers scrabbled for a hold on the gritty shingles, but she was sliding too fast and the shingles slipped from her grasp. Her legs went over the edge of the roof. Then her elbows hit something sharp. She stretched her fingers out again and wrapped them around the lip of the gutter.

Livvie's eyes had been open the whole time, the endless three seconds it took for her to slide down and over the edge of the roof. But now she closed them. She knew she was going to fall. The gutter was old and rusted. It was going to break off and she was going to fall straight down to the cement patio. She wondered if the cat was still watching.

Somebody was screaming.

It took a second for Livvie to realize it was her own voice. When she did, when she knew she hadn't fallen yet, she opened her eyes and screamed again.

It seemed like forever until she heard a voice say, "I'm coming, Livvie. I'm coming."

But it wasn't the voice she wanted to hear.

It was Richardson's voice.

Livvie looked up and saw her stepfather sitting on the roof inching his way down to her. After telling her he was coming, he didn't say anything else. She couldn't see his face, but she didn't need to.

He wasn't coming to help her, he was coming to push her the rest of the way off.

He was coming to kill her.

"This is perfect, isn't it?!" she sobbed. "You'll try to save me but you won't be able to!"

He didn't say anything, just kept moving toward her. She knew what he was thinking. He wouldn't have to fake a suicide now. He'd pry her fingers up, or step on them, or push the gutter loose. This was a made-to-order tragedy, a perfect way to get rid of the stepdaughter who'd stumbled across his secret.

It would only take him a few seconds. Nobody else was around, nobody else would see what really happened. Joel should be there, but he wasn't. Where was he? Where was Joel?

Richardson was closer. He'd shifted his weight, and he was stretching his arm out toward her. "Livvie," he said. "Let go."

Livvie could see his face now. It was calm and still. He wasn't even frowning.

But it was his eyes that scared her the most. His light brown eyes were open wide, looking straight into hers. She could see them shining with some kind of feeling. Not fear. Not anger.

They were shining with triumph.

"Let go and give me your hand," he said.

She could feel the gutter cutting into her skin. Her nails were sunk into mud and matted leaves, but her palms were stinging and she knew they must be bleeding. She wanted nothing more than to let go and reach out. But not to Richardson's deadly hand.

"Joel!" she cried. "Joel!"

"Let go, Livvie," Richardson said, his eyes still glinting. "I'm here. I'll do it."

"Joel!" Livvie screamed again, and then she heard Joel's voice answering her.

"Go on, Livvie!" Joel shouted. "Take his hand!"

Livvie couldn't see him, but she knew he could see her. Joel could see her, so Richardson couldn't do what he wanted. Not now. "He can't do it!" she cried.

"Yes he can, Livvie!" Joel shouted. "Trust me!"

Livvie looked at Richardson. His face hadn't changed. But the light was going out of his eyes.

He'd lost.

This time, he'd lost and he knew it, and his eyes were flat and defeated. With a sound somewhere between a laugh and a sob, Livvie let go of the gutter, stretched her arm up, and felt his hand closing over hers.

Chapter 20

The ladder had slipped along the edge of the roof, but it was still standing. After Allen Richardson pulled Livvie up to safety, Joel scooted down the roof and straightened the ladder, then climbed down to the patio. "Okay!" he called up. "I've got it steady. Come on down, Livvie."

"Let her catch her breath first," Richardson said.

"No." Livvie pushed her hair out of her eyes with the back of her hand. "I want to go down now."

"Livvie, you're shaking," Richardson said soothingly. "Just take a few seconds and — "

"I want to go down," Livvie said again. She wished she could scream it at him but she didn't have enough breath left. They were sitting with their feet braced against the gutter. Richardson had his hand around Livvie's arm and when she rolled aside to get onto her knees, his hand slipped down and caught her wrist. She looked at him and he smiled. "Go ahead. I'll hold you until your feet are steady on the ladder."

Livvie inched backwards and felt for the top of the ladder with her toes. Soon she was off the roof completely, her head just above the gutter. She looked up at Richardson again. "It almost worked, didn't it?"

"What?" He started to say something else. Then he just shook his head. "Go on down, Livvie."

She shouldn't have said it, Livvie thought, as she made her way down the ladder. It sounded crazy. Richardson knew what she was talking about, but he pretended not to. He'd report it to her mother, naturally, and it would be one more piece of evidence that Livvie was falling apart.

When she reached the bottom rung, Joel put his arm around her shoulder and she stepped off onto the solid concrete of the patio. She leaned against him for a few seconds. "Thanks," she finally whispered.

His arm tightened. "I'm glad you're okay. But I didn't have anything to do with it."

Livvie drew away and looked up. Richardson was turning around now, getting ready to come down. "You had more to do with it than you think," she said to Joel. She turned and headed for the door. The cat was still on the patio wall.

"Whose cat?" Livvie asked.

"What?" Joel looked startled, like he wasn't expecting that kind of question from someone who'd almost fallen off a roof. "The cat? He's the neighbor's," he said. "He's a beast."

"I like him." The cat flicked its tail and Livvie smiled a little. Maybe it was a salute — one survivor to another.

Livvie was washing her hands in the kitchen when Joel came in. He opened a cabinet and took down a can of antiseptic spray. When Livvie finished patting her hands dry with paper towels, he held each hand gently and sprayed it. "Not too bad," he said. "Just scratches mostly. You want Band-Aids?"

She shook her head.

"Livvie — "

"Where's Richardson?" she interrupted.

"Putting the ladder away, I think." Joel set the can on the counter. "Livvie, what happened up there?"

"I slipped."

"I figured that," he said. "But I meant later. When you wouldn't let go of the gutter."

Livvie had been tugging the crowbar out of her belt loop. When it came free, she slammed it down on the kitchen table. "Do you really have to ask me that, after what I told you this morning?"

Joel started to say something, but Livvie didn't let him. "You don't believe me," she said. "I know you don't believe me and I guess I can't blame you. But don't expect me to stand here and listen while you tell me he saved my life and I should be grateful. *You* saved my life, okay? If you hadn't been there — " she broke off. "I have to get out of here."

"What?"

Livvie was already at the door. "I have to get out of here," she said again. "I'm going home."

Leaving Joel standing in the kitchen, Livvie ran up the stairs. She wasn't going to pack, all she needed was her purse, with some money and her driver's license in it. She started for the back stairs, then turned around, ran to Joanne's room and got the cordless phone. She'd call Marta first. If she hadn't mailed the newspaper articles yet, she'd tell her not to. Knowing Marta, Livvie thought there was a good chance she hadn't sent them. If she had, there was nothing Livvie could do about it. She wasn't going to wait around for them to get here.

She should have left days ago. She should

never have come in the first place.

She wasn't safe, not with her stepfather around.

In her room, Livvie shut the door and slid down to the floor, punching Marta's number. She leaned against the door and waited while the phone rang.

Marta's mother picked up on the sixth ring. She sounded tired. "Mrs. Ryland, this is Livvie. Is Marta there?"

Livvie heard Marta's mother sigh. "I'm afraid not, Livvie," she said. "Marta wanted me to call you, but I just got back from the hospital and haven't had a chance to find the number."

"The hospital?" Livvie tightened her grip on the phone and winced as the scratches stung. "What happened?"

"Well, I'm still not sure of all the details," Mrs. Ryland said. "But Marta's going to be fine."

"*Marta's* in the hospital? What happened?" Livvie asked again.

"She had a dentist's appointment this morning," Mrs. Ryland said. "And she'd parked the car in the underground lot — you know the place, your family goes to the same dentist."

"Yes."

"Well, Marta said she'd just gotten out of

the car and was starting to walk to the elevator. All of a sudden another car came barreling out of nowhere it seemed like, and just . . . just drove straight at her, she said." Mrs. Ryland's voice caught in her throat and she took a second to calm down. "Well, Marta didn't have much time to react, of course. She was so lucky."

"You mean the car hit her?"

"On the side," Mrs. Ryland said. "It all happened so fast. She heard it and she said she just saw it out of the corner of her eye. And she was moving to get out of the way, so it didn't hit her full on. When she fell, she banged her head pretty badly. In fact, she was unconscious for a while, nobody knows how long. The doctor wants her to stay in the hospital overnight, just for observation, she says."

"Thank God she's okay," Livvie said. "What about the car? I mean, what did the driver have to say?"

"The driver didn't have anything to say," Marta's mother said, "because the driver didn't stick around! The garage attendant found Marta, but he was on his break when it happened and nobody else was around to see the car. It was a hit-and-run, Livvie. I still can't believe it."

Livvie suddenly went cold.

A hit-and-run, yes. But not an accident.

She knew. She knew who'd been driving that car.

"Mrs. Ryland, I'm coming home," Livvie said. She looked at her watch. Four o'clock. She could be there by five-thirty or six at the latest. "I want to go see Marta, will that be okay?"

"Of course," Mrs. Ryland said. "She's going to be fine, really. She doesn't even want to be there, so I know she'll be glad to see you."

Marta's mother gave Livvie the name of the hospital and the room number, and they said good-bye. Livvie got her purse and hurried down the stairs and out the front door. Joel was coming around the corner of the house as she went out. She heard him call her name, but she didn't stop. She got in her mother's car, gunned the engine, and drove down the driveway. Kyle was just pulling in on his motorcycle, but Livvie didn't slow down. Kyle swerved to the side, a look of surprise and outrage on his face.

Once she was out of Cliffside and on the highway heading home, Livvie relaxed, a little. Richardson didn't even know she'd gone. Once he found out, he could hardly come tearing after her.

She was safe for a while.

Livvie's hands hurt where she gripped the

steering wheel, but she didn't pay much attention. She was too busy thinking about Marta. Everybody in the house had heard the message Marta left yesterday — that she was going to the dentist this morning and would go to the post office right after that.

But only two people knew what it meant: Livvie and Richardson. Richardson had left early this morning, and he knew where to find Marta because they went to the same dentist.

He'd gone there and waited for her.

He must have been after the newspaper articles, Livvie thought. She wondered if he'd gotten them. He might have taken them from Marta's car when she was unconscious. But even if he'd found them, Livvie was still a threat to him and he knew it. He must have hated pulling her back onto that roof. Joel had ruined a perfect opportunity for him.

Richardson must be feeling desperate by now. All these years, he must have been looking for recognition in a stranger's eyes.

He never thought he'd be found out by his own stepdaughter.

Marta had a bruise on her cheek and a bandage on her elbow. Except for that, she looked fine. "Be glad you can't see my left hip," she said after Livvie commented on how good she looked. "It has this humongous bruise on it. I hope it's gone before I have to put on a swimsuit."

"So why are they keeping you here?" Livvie asked.

"Oh, the doctor said I have a slight concussion," Marta said. "She wants to make sure I don't start frothing at the mouth or something. It's boring. All the male doctors are duds. How come they're always gorgeous on television?"

Livvie laughed. "Maybe you'll find a cute intern. Um . . . Marta. Did you see who hit you?"

"The police asked me that about a thousand times," Marta said. "But I was too busy jumping out of the way."

"Well, I'm really glad you're all right."

"Me, too." Marta looked at her curiously. "Why did you come back, anyway?"

"To see you, why do you think?" Livvie said. "I called and your mother told me what happened."

"I bet I know why you called, too. The envelope, right?" Marta lay back against her pillows and sighed. "Livvie, I'm sorry, but I didn't mail it."

"Of course, Marta, how could you have? You got hit by a car, remember?"

"No, I mean I didn't even take it with me," Marta explained. "I meant to, I really did. But I forgot. It's still at home."

"Well, don't feel guilty!" Livvie said. "If anyone should feel guilty, it's me."

"Why?"

"Because, if it hadn't been for that envelope — " Livvie stopped. She didn't know if Marta would believe her, but whether or not she did, there was no sense getting her upset when she'd been hurt. "Never mind," she said. "I don't know what I'm talking about. Listen, the nurse gave me a dirty look when I got here because visiting hours are almost over. I'm going to go before she throws me out, but I'll call you tomorrow, okay?"

"Be sure to call me at home, not here," Marta reminded her. "But wait — are you going back to Cliffside?"

"No," Livvie said, and when Marta started to ask a question, she added, "I can't explain now. But I will. I'll be able to explain everything, soon."

After stopping off at Marta's house to pick up the envelope, Livvie drove home and let herself into the house. A couple of lamps were on, set on a timer Richardson had rigged up. But the house still felt different, smaller, the way it always did when she'd been away.

Livvie went into the kitchen and sat down, the envelope on the table in front of her. Her hands shook a little as she ripped off the tape Marta had used, then pulled out the second envelope, the one from the newspaper.

It's in here, she thought, tearing open the second envelope. Somewhere in here she was going to find the key that would open the lock to Allen Richardson's past.

Chapter 21

Livvie pulled out several sheets of paper, clipped together with a bill on top. She took off the paperclip and pushed the bill aside.

The articles had been photocopied, and she spent a couple of minutes getting them in order, her eyes scanning them as she did. Finally, she was ready to read.

The first story was about the fire, of course, and the deaths of Sharon and Cynthia Clinton. There were pictures of them, blurry and indistinct because of the copying. The only thing the story said about Adam Clinton was that he hadn't been notified yet. Livvie went impatiently to the next article.

This one made the front page, too, and the headline read, *Questions Raised About Clinton Fire; Husband Being Sought*. But the article didn't tell Livvie anything about Adam Clinton himself.

After two more articles, which told about the life insurance, described how the fire had been set and how Clinton had disappeared and was wanted for questioning in the deaths of his wife and stepdaughter, the stories finally started going into detail about Adam Clinton himself.

Livvie's eyes raced down the pages, looking for anything that would tie Clinton to Richardson. *"He seemed like a nice guy,"* one of his co-workers said. *"He wasn't a big talker, he kind of kept to himself, but that's no crime. I just can't believe it, even though it looks like it's true."*

"He was the kind of man you just didn't pay much attention to," his boss was quoted as saying. *"He did his job well, and that's all I was interested in."*

Another co-worker said he thought Clinton was a little strange because he never talked much about his family. *"Most of us talked about our wives and kids, but he didn't say much. I thought he was a little cold, standoffish, but maybe that's hindsight."*

Livvie shifted in her chair, feeling frustrated. She was looking for something specific, like the glasses, or a hobby, the eyebrows — anything. But Clinton's parents were dead and he didn't have brothers or sisters. He'd gone to high school in Ohio. He'd been in the army late in the Vietnam War, but he didn't fight, and nobody remembered him anyway. Sharon Clinton's friends said she seemed happy with him, that he was nice. They said they didn't really know him.

Nobody really knows him except me, Livvie thought. She started shuffling the papers together, planning to go over them again, just in case she'd missed something.

Then she saw the photograph.

It was like all the other photos, black and fuzzy. She hadn't looked at it closely before. But now she did.

The picture was of two men, standing together. One of the men was Richardson. She was sure of it. His head was tilted and his eyebrows were raised. His hands were blurred, so she couldn't see any birthmark. But she didn't have to. The man was her stepfather.

Livvie stared at the picture for a few seconds. Then her eyes slid down to the caption underneath. At first, she didn't think she was reading right. She read it again.

This time she felt a jolt, as if she'd been hit. She realized she hadn't read the caption wrong.

And she knew without any doubt that she'd been right all along.

The caption read, *Adam Clinton and an*

army friend, Allen Richardson, who died in Vietnam.

Livvie wanted to laugh. She wanted to cry and scream and laugh all at the same time.

Allen Richardson had died. He had died and her stepfather knew it. So he just took his name and part of his background, because who would ever question him? Who would ever guess that so many years later, his stepdaughter would call up Chesterfield high? Of course they had a record of Allen Richardson. He went there.

But the real Allen Richardson had been dead for years.

Her stepfather *was* Adam Clinton.

Livvie was still staring at the photograph when she heard the sound of a footstep behind her.

Chapter 22

The light went out in the kitchen. Livvie stumbled up from her chair. But even as she did, she felt an arm slide around her neck from behind, pressing hard against her throat. She brought her hands up and dug her nails into the arm, but he was wearing gloves, and something with long sleeves. She wasn't hurting him at all.

She kicked back, but only succeeded in kicking the chair over. Her hands were still on his arms, and she tried to pull the sleeve up so she could scrape him with her nails. But now his other arm was around her chest and she was having trouble breathing.

She wanted to scream, but she couldn't take a deep enough breath. All that came out was a high-pitched squeal. Livvie let go of his arm and reached up behind her, for his face. She wanted to rake her nails across his face and make *him* scream.

Instead of skin, she felt cloth. A ski mask. He was wearing a ski mask. Livvie tugged at the knitted material, trying to pull it off his head, but he just leaned his head away and she couldn't do it. She was pinned against him and she felt his stomach move in and out against her back. He was laughing.

Enraged, Livvie grabbed his arm again, and this time she was able to pull his sleeve up. She could feel his flesh under her fingers. She bent her head and sank her teeth into the tender skin on the inside of his wrist.

He didn't scream. But she heard him gasp and she knew she'd hurt him. He pulled his arm away a little. She tried to move. She tried to slip down, but he tightened his arm around her throat and she couldn't.

Furious, terrified, Livvie lifted her hands again. Like claws, her fingers grabbed hold of his ski mask. She wasn't going to let go this time.

She could feel his skin beneath it and she dug her fingers in as hard as she could. Pinching. Clawing. Twisting.

He hissed through his teeth and Livvie knew she was hurting him. It gave her strength. She kicked back again and missed. Desperate, she brought her leg up and stomped down hard on his foot. She dug her fingers into his face, and this time, he pulled away.

With every bit of strength she had, Livvie thrashed back and forth, twisting in his arms. She felt the mask slip up, and she tightened her hold. With another burst of energy, she twisted around until she was facing him. Gasping for breath, she dragged the ski mask off and spun away from him, putting the table between them.

The kitchen was dark; the lights from the living room didn't reach in here.

But Livvie didn't need bright lights to see Allen Richardson's face. He stood four feet away from her, with only the table between them.

"I knew it was you," she said as she faced him across the table. "And I know what you wanted to do. You were going to kill me and make it look like a suicide."

He didn't say anything. He didn't move.

"I know who you are!" Livvie shouted. "You're Adam Clinton!"

Finally, Allen Richardson nodded. "You're very clever, Livvie. It's really too bad."

Livvie didn't take her eyes off of him.

"I'm curious," he said. "I know you figured

it out. But how? What got you started in the first place?"

"Television." Livvie said. "I saw you on television. *Fugitives from Justice*. You're famous."

He shook his head. "Adam Clinton's famous. Not Allen Richardson."

He was going to try to kill her. Livvie knew it. She wanted to run, but he'd catch her before she got two feet away. She made herself stay still.

"I'll bet you wish you'd never seen that show," Richardson said. "Just think, Livvie, if you'd never seen it, everything would have been fine."

Livvie's mind was racing. "How did you find out I knew?" she asked. "It was the phone, wasn't it? You listened in when I called Marta from Cliffside."

"Well, I thought you were acting kind of strange even before that," Richardson said. "You've always been cool to me, so when you started asking questions about my past, I was curious. On the alert, I guess you'd say. But yes, I really knew when I listened in on the phone. Then I found your notebook." He shook his head again. "You should have been more careful, Livvie."

"You hit Marta, didn't you?" Livvie said. "You were actually willing to kill my friend just to keep me from getting those newspaper stories." She gestured at the floor where the articles had been scattered during their struggle. "You broke the banister. And shut me in the basement and snuck into my room. You were trying to make everybody think I was breaking down again."

"It was working, too."

"It won't work now," Livvie said. "I was right, wasn't I? You were going to kill me here and make it look like suicide. But it won't work now. I'll fight. You'll have to hit me. It'll show. It'll show when they find me and nobody will think I killed myself."

"Well, you'll never know. Will you, Livvie?"

Richardson moved then, swiftly lunging forward and shoving the table at Livvie. It hit her in the thighs and she fell back against the counter. Now he was coming after her, climbing up on the table. Livvie tried to slide underneath it, but he saw what she was doing and leaped off, pushing the table again and pinning her to the counter.

Livvie felt the edge of the counter digging into her back. She reached behind her and swept one hand back and forth, trying to find something to throw at him. Her hand hit the knife holder, a cube-shaped block of wood with slits for the blades.

A gift to her mother from her stepfather.

Livvie's fingers closed around a knife handle. She knocked the wooden block over and slid the knife out.

She swung it at him just as he lunged across the table again.

The tip of the blade caught him on the side of the face.

He stopped moving. Livvie saw a jagged gash in his skin. It was white, then it quickly reddened as the blood started seeping out. Shocked and sickened, she watched it trail down his face like a wash of red paint.

Slowly, Richardson brought his hand up to his face. He looked at the blood on his fingertips. Then he looked at Livvie. His eyes were bright, murderous.

Livvie raised the knife. "I'll do it!" she cried. "Don't think I won't!" She meant it. If he came at her again, she'd kill him.

Richardson didn't move. But he didn't back off, either. Livvie's breath was coming in sobs and her hand was shaking. "Get out!" she cried. "Get out of here!"

Richardson moved then. He moved toward her. Livvie raised the knife higher and opened her mouth to scream.

Suddenly, the front doorbell rang. Livvie jumped at the sound. She didn't drop the knife, but she jumped.

Richardson was off the table in a flash. When his feet hit the floor, he shoved the table against her once more, hard. Then he turned and ran out the back door.

The doorbell rang again. Then somebody pounded on the front door. Sobbing, Livvie shoved the table away and locked the back door. Then she went out of the kitchen, down the hall, and turned on the porch light. She carried the knife with her.

Joel was standing on the small front porch, his dark brown eyes wide and worried. Livvie pulled the door open.

"Olivia. Livvie," he said. He looked down, at the knife. There was blood on the tip. He looked back up to her face.

"It was Richardson," Livvie told him. "He was here. He tried to kill me. He ran out when you rang the doorbell. He was going to kill me!"

Joel stepped quickly inside and put his hand on her shoulders. "Are you all right?"

"No. Yes."

"You said he left when I rang," Joel said. He looked down the hall, worried. "Will he come back? I mean, do you think he's still out there?"

Livvie shook her head. "He wouldn't come back now. He knows somebody else is here. That wasn't part of his plan. He just wanted me, and it's too late for that now."

Joel pulled her close and held her for a moment. It felt wonderful. "How come you're here?" Livvie asked.

"I don't know. I mean, you were so upset and then you ran out of there." Joel stepped back and looked at her again. "I just had to make sure you were all right."

Livvie managed a smile. "Too bad you didn't get here a little sooner." She leaned against him again, then straightened up and took his hand. "Come on," she said. "I'll show you."

In the kitchen, Joel helped her pick up the scattered newspaper articles and slide the table back. They sat down, and he watched silently while Livvie searched through the papers until she found the one she wanted.

"Look at this." She pointed to the photograph.

"My God," Joel said. "That's *him*."

Livvie pointed to the caption underneath. "See? Adam Clinton and Allen Richardson. They were in the army together, but Allen Richardson died in Vietnam. Remember I told you about Chesterfield high?"

Joel nodded. "You said you couldn't explain it." He took the paper from her hand. "But this does. He just used the guy's name. I thought . . . "

"You thought I was crazy," Livvie said. "That's okay. I don't blame you. I was starting to think that, too. Some of the time anyway."

"I didn't think you were crazy, Livvie." Joel sounded angry. "Just because you had a breakdown or whatever didn't make me think you were bonkers. Give me a break, okay? I'm not that much of a jerk." He blew out a breath and almost glared at her.

"I never said you were even a little bit of a jerk." Livvie smiled. "But you thought I was wrong, didn't you?"

"Yeah, I thought you were wrong," Joel admitted. "It just seemed too wild."

Livvie smiled again. She really didn't blame him. It *was* wild. She thought of something. "How'd you know where I lived?"

"Your mother," he said. "When she and Mom got home, I told them where you'd gone."

"Was Richardson there?"

"He'd already left," Joel said. "But I didn't see him go. Anyway, I got directions from your mother."

"We have to go back," Livvie said. She stood

up. "I have to tell her what happened. I have to tell her everything before I tell anyone else."

Before they left, Joel called to let their mothers know they were on their way home. Joanne said that Richardson had left abruptly for a business meeting and hadn't returned yet. The rest of the family was going out with some neighbors to grab dinner and would see them later.

Joel had a hundred questions for Livvie and on the drive back to Cliffside, Livvie told him about Marta and everything else that had happened. He kept his eyes on the road, but every once in a while he reached over and squeezed her hand.

A light rain started as they drove through the night, and when Livvie finished talking and Joel stopped asking questions, she listened to the patter on the roof and felt her eyes get heavy and her head droop forward. By the time they reached Cliffside, she was sound asleep.

She woke to the touch of a hand on her hair. It was soft and light as a feather, but she jerked awake in an instant. A scream died in her throat when she heard Joel's voice. "It's okay, Livvie," he said. "We're home. His car's not here. It's okay."

Livvie sat up straight, rubbed her face and eyes and looked out the window. The front porch light was on, looking like a beacon in the rain. She wondered where Richardson was. Had he just taken off, disappeared, the way he had so many years ago?

Livvie and Joel ran through the rain and up the steps into the house. Once inside Livvie kept hold of Joel's hand. "Would you come up to my room with me?"

"Sure. But he's not there, Livvie," Joel said.

"I know. But I'm still afraid," Livvie said. "I keep remembering things he did. I'm afraid to be alone."

The room was empty. Nothing looked out of place. The phone was still on the bed where Livvie had tossed it earlier. Livvie went to the bed and sat down. Eerily, the minute she did, the phone rang. Livvie jumped and picked it up. She slid the button to talk and said hello.

"Hello, Livvie," Allen Richardson said.

Livvie froze. "It's him," she whispered.

Joel stared at her, his eyes wide and startled.

"You were lucky," Richardson said to Livvie. "Do you know how lucky you were?"

"I know," Livvie held the phone tight, shuddering at the sound of his voice. "Where are you?"

"You don't really expect me to answer that," Richardson said. "I don't have much time. I called for a reason."

Livvie waited.

"Tell your mother good-bye for me," he said. "And Livvie?"

"Yes?"

"If we meet again, you won't be so lucky. Remember that." There was a click. Richardson had hung up.

Livvie dropped the phone and stood up.

"What did he say?" Joel asked. "He's gone, isn't he? He's not coming back."

Livvie nodded, tears starting in her eyes. "He said I wouldn't be lucky if we met again."

"He won't come after you." Joel put his arms around her and pulled her close. "He'll never be back," he said. "He wouldn't dare. He's gone off somewhere and he'll never come back here. You're safe now."

"Yes." A couple of tears dripped from Livvie's chin onto his shirt, but she didn't move. Soon she'd have to tell her mother. And the police. She'd probably be telling hundreds of people in the days to come. But the telling could wait, just a little while longer.

Epilogue

"Honey!" Mrs. Landsman's voice called from the bottom of the stairs. "Come on down, we don't have much time before the movie starts!"

Rebecca closed her book and scooted backwards off the bed. On the back of her closet door was a full-length mirror, and she stopped and checked herself in front of it. She probably should have changed into a different shirt; this one was all wrinkled from lying down. But there wasn't time. She combed her hair back with her fingers and hurried out of the room.

Her mother was waiting in the entryway, smiling a little nervously. "Here you are!" she said brightly. "Come say hello."

There was a man standing behind her mother. She'd been expecting to meet him. Her mother had been talking about him for days. He was kind of average-looking, not tall, not short. His hair was light brown, and his eyebrows, just a shade darker, were raised, like he was surprised at something.

He had a close-clipped beard, but there was a scar on his cheek, and the hair grew around it. The small patch of shiny white scar tissue was jagged, like a bolt of lightning.

He smiled at her and said hello, and Rebecca smiled back. He looked like a nice man.

About the Author

Carol Ellis is the author of more than fifteen books for young people, including *The Window*, *My Secret Admirer*, and the short story, "The Doll" in *Thirteen*. While she doesn't read horror books herself, some of her favorite reading is mystery and suspense, especially those books in which an ordinary, innocent person becomes caught up in something strange and frightening.

Carol Ellis lives in New York State with her husband and their son.

point®

THRILLERS

R.L. Stine

- ❏ MC44236-8 The Baby-sitter — $3.50
- ❏ MC44332-1 The Baby-sitter II — $3.50
- ❏ MC45386-6 Beach House — $3.25
- ❏ MC43278-8 Beach Party — $3.50
- ❏ MC43125-0 Blind Date — $3.50
- ❏ MC43279-6 The Boyfriend — $3.50
- ❏ MC44333-X The Girlfriend — $3.50
- ❏ MC45385-8 Hit and Run — $3.25
- ❏ MC46100-1 The Hitchhiker — $3.50
- ❏ MC43280-X The Snowman — $3.50
- ❏ MC43139-0 Twisted — $3.50

Caroline B. Cooney

- ❏ MC44316-X The Cheerleader — $3.25
- ❏ MC41641-3 The Fire — $3.25
- ❏ MC43806-9 The Fog — $3.25
- ❏ MC45681-4 Freeze Tag — $3.25
- ❏ MC45402-1 The Perfume — $3.25
- ❏ MC44884-6 The Return of the Vampire — $2.95
- ❏ MC41640-5 The Snow — $3.25
- ❏ MC45682-2 The Vampire's Promise — $3.50

Diane Hoh

- ❏ MC44330-5 The Accident — $3.25
- ❏ MC45401-3 The Fever — $3.25
- ❏ MC43050-5 Funhouse — $3.25
- ❏ MC44904-4 The Invitation — $3.50
- ❏ MC45640-7 The Train (9/92) — $3.25

Sinclair Smith

- ❏ MC45063-8 The Waitress — $2.95

Christopher Pike

- ❏ MC43014-9 Slumber Party — $3.50
- ❏ MC44256-2 Weekend — $3.50

A. Bates

- ❏ MC45829-9 The Dead Game — $3.25
- ❏ MC43291-5 Final Exam — $3.25
- ❏ MC44582-0 Mother's Helper — $3.50
- ❏ MC44238-4 Party Line — $3.25

D.E. Athkins

- ❏ MC45246-0 Mirror, Mirror — $3.25
- ❏ MC45349-1 The Ripper — $3.25
- ❏ MC44941-9 Sister Dearest — $2.95

Carol Ellis

- ❏ MC44768-8 My Secret Admirer — $3.25
- ❏ MC46044-7 The Stepdaughter — $3.25
- ❏ MC44916-8 The Window — $2.95

Richie Tankersley Cusick

- ❏ MC43115-3 April Fools — $3.25
- ❏ MC43203-6 The Lifeguard — $3.25
- ❏ MC43114-5 Teacher's Pet — $3.25
- ❏ MC44235-X Trick or Treat — $3.25

Lael Littke

- ❏ MC44237-6 Prom Dress — $3.25

Edited by T. Pines

- ❏ MC45256-8 Thirteen — $3.50

Available wherever you buy books, or use this order form.

Scholastic Inc., P.O. Box 7502, 2931 East McCarty Street, Jefferson City, MO 65102

Please send me the books I have checked above. I am enclosing $_____ (please add $2.00 to cover shipping and handling). Send check or money order — no cash or C.O.D.s please.

Name _____

Address_____

City_____ State/Zip_____

Please allow four to six weeks for delivery. Offer good in the U.S. only. Sorry, mail orders are not available to residents of Canada. Prices subject to change.   PT1092